For the Love of Amanda

For the Love of Amanda

For the Love of Amanda

JACQUELINE DEGROOT

RED LEAF
BOOKS

AN IMPRINT OF OCTOBER PUBLISHING
WILMINGTON, NC

Book and Jacket Design by October Publishing.

ISBN: 0-9747374-2-9

Applied for Library of Congress Cataloging-in-Publication Data.

09 08 07 06 05 04   6 5 4 3 2 1

Printed in the United States.

A Very Big Thank You To My Proofreaders:

My aerobics partner and good friend, Kathy Blaine;
My neighbor and ever-efficient editor, Arlene Cook;
My wonderful, inspiring sister, Jean Dean;
My loving, supportive husband, Bill DeGroot;
My champagne buddy, Deanna Eirtle;
My most incredible mom, Regina Flemion;
My greatest source of encouragement, Peggy Grich;
My Florida fishing pal, Beth Howard;
My fellow, avid, romance reader, Martha Murphy;
and
My very first fan, Barbara Scott-Cannon.

To my mother, Regina, who epitomizes the very word nurturing. Her love truly knows no bounds. I was blessed when I was chosen to be her child.

BEFORE I FORMED YOU IN THE WOMB I KNEW YOU.

JEREMIAH 1:5

It's bad, Gabby. It's not going away. There doesn't seem to be anything they can do for me anymore. They think I'm going to die."

"Oh, Mandy! This is so hard for me. How hard must it be for *you*? I don't know how you're coping, I seriously don't." Gabby was wringing her hands between her thighs, scratching white lines with her fingernails into her dark indigo jeans.

"I think I've kind of known it was going to end up this way for a long time. I've kind of accepted it. But it's really hard on my mom. She's devastated, she doesn't know what to do. She was okay when we had some hope. When we were doing the treatments, things were much, much better. But since we got the test results yesterday, she's been in a shell, afraid to come out."

"How long are they saying you have before you relapse this time?"

"This year sometime, unless there's a miracle. Mom's on the computer now, trying to dial one up," she added with a small chuckle.

"She won't give up Mandy, you know that."

"I know. This is so much harder on her than it is on anyone else."

"You're her baby. Her only baby. You're all she has."

"I know. She says that all the time and it's starting to grate on me."

"Well, let's not dwell on it. Let's find ways to have some fun, to take your mind down to the vegging-out level. How about a movie and a sleep over? Mom's fixing tacos for dinner. You couldn't eat them before, but now you can."

"Yeah, I can for a while. Sounds good. Let me go ask Mom."

Together the two girls got up off the front stoop and went into the large Victorian house with the wraparound front porch. They found Mandy's mom just where Mandy had said she'd be, in front of the computer.

Ever since Mandy had been diagnosed, Michele Moore had been frantically looking for the cure. Every newspaper article, every web site, every hotline was researched completely in hopes that it would lead to the answer.

"Mom, is it okay if I eat dinner at the Grissen's, then go to the movies and spend the night with Gabby?"

Michele looked up and smiled. "Sure, honey. Just make sure you keep warm and don't share your popcorn. Remember you can't afford a cold or the flu right now. That'll give me a chance to do some more research on-line."

Mandy bent over and gave her mom a kiss on the cheek. "Don't work too hard on this Mom, it's probably not going to pan out. I've accepted it. Why can't you?"

Michele wrapped her arms around Mandy and tears filled her eyes. "I just can't. You're my little girl, you're all I've got. I have to look out for you the best I can."

"I'm not so little, Mom. I'm sixteen."

"Yes, I know exactly how old you are. I was there when you were born remember?" she chided. "It was a frosty cold morning. I didn't even want to get out of bed, but you kept kicking me. I thought you were trying to kick your way out. I made it to the hospital with only forty minutes to spare."

"And Daddy came right from the airport, just in time to see me wail," Mandy added with a sheepish smile. It was a story she'd been told often over the years.

The mention of her father sobered them all up. It was still hard for Michele to believe he was gone; that he'd died six years ago piloting a commercial jetliner that had been improperly designed. For a handful of better quality and more strategically-placed rivets, her husband, and Mandy's father would still be here today. He would be here helping her deal with this latest round of bad news.

"C'mon Mandy, let's go," Gabby said as she tried to pull her along. She knew what it was like when Mandy and her mom were reminded of her dad. "'Bye Mrs. Moore. Mom will call you tonight."

"'Bye Gabby. You girls be good. And no R-rated movies, you hear?"

"Yes, Mom, we know."

And how they knew! Mandy thought. Her Mom harped about sex and violence in the movies all the time. She was a really nice lady, but one of the strictest moms on the planet as far as Gabby and Mandy were concerned.

While the girls watched *Maid In Manhattan* at the local mall and munched on popcorn and gummy bears, Michele Moore surfed the Web.

She took a break to reheat some leftover roast pork lo mein and to make a pot of her favorite Chai tea. Then she was back again on her iMac. She was trying desperately to find the clue that would cure her daughter's illness. She knew without a doubt that the answer was there, she just wasn't sure that she'd find it in time. And now they were running out of time.

God, how awful she felt in the doctor's office yesterday when he told them the news. The feeling of dread she felt at that moment was worse than the dread she lived with after they called about Kevin's plane crashing. She had just begun to drag herself up out of the mire of that, when Mandy had fallen sick.

Juvenile Myelomonocyctic Leukemia . . . curable to a point, but then steadily debilitating once a relapse occurred. And she relapsed in June, right after the school year. What an awful summer they had.

Thank God they didn't have to worry about money. The airline had been generous, thanks to her attorney, and what was even better was the survivor's benefits allowing her to keep their hospitalization. The money spent on Mandy's treatment was well into the hundreds of thousands. By the time this was all over, they would top a million for sure. No doubt about it. And that was if she died. If she lived, who knew?

Michele's fingers clicked on the mouse and she followed window after window as new links opened with more information. It was ten o'clock and her eyes were getting tired when she stumbled onto a web site detailing umbilical cord blood research regarding Juvenile Myelomonocyctic Leukemia. Her eyes flew across the page as she tried to absorb everything. She read it again, and again. Then she printed darned near the whole damned site. Could it be? Could you really do this?

She turned off the computer, grabbed her mug of now-cold tea, took the printed papers off the printer ledge and went to her bedroom. Then she sat up in bed reading everything all over again until two in the morning.

From what she was reading, if what she was reading was true, Mandy's best chance for survival would be if they could develop an injection made from umbilical cord cells taken from a sibling. Rich cells that came from the umbilical cord that was routinely discarded after a baby's birth. Mandy had no sibling. Even if she did, they wouldn't have thought to save the cord. However, another idea tumbled around in Michele's head until she finally had to say it out loud just to find out if it sounded as crazy to her ears as it did floating around in her head. *I could have another baby. I could have a baby for Mandy.*

Yes, it sounded crazy. Absolutely! She dropped the papers to the floor and took another sip of her tea. *Would she ever get to drink it hot again?* She turned off the bedside lamp, then she turned on her side and faced Kevin's side of the bed. She always did that when she was troubled. At times, she actually talked to his pillow. But this time, she knew what she was thinking was nuts! And he'd probably tell her so if he could. As she stared past the bed and out the window, she saw the porch lights on Gabby's house go out. She knew they were on a timer and apparently it was now 2:13 A.M.

She let her mind wander, hoping it would purge some things so she could actually get some sleep tonight. Last night, she hadn't been able to sleep at all. Magically, she fell asleep, which allowed her subconscious to take over her troubles for a while.

"That was a great movie," Gabby whispered to Mandy who was in the bed next to hers. "Makes you believe that even a maid can find her Prince Charming . . . just like Cinderella."

"Yeah. But you should always be who you are. It's too hard to carry off anything else."

"It was nice of her friends to try to help her though, and her son."

"That's what friends do."

"I wish that I could find a way to help you."

"Maybe you can."

"How?" Gabby asked, forcing herself up on her elbow, her eyes bright with hope.

"I've got an idea bouncing around in my head. Let me think it over for a while, see if it gels. Let's get some sleep. We'll talk tomorrow."

"Okay. 'Night."

"You can say 'good' night, you know."

"Nothin's going to be 'good' until you're better. Face it. I'm not sayin' 'good' night, 'good' morning, or 'good' afternoon anymore."

"God, you're stubborn!"

When Michele woke early the next morning, she refrained from moving. She was afraid if she moved, she would forget everything that had come into her head in the middle of the night. Everything she had said to Kevin and everything he had said to her.

Her hand reached out to stroke his pillow and she whispered, "I have to do all I can to save her Kevin, I know that's what you would want. And I know that right now you'd be doing everything in your power to make me pregnant so we could save our little girl. Now just tell me how I can save her."

Her head lifted a little off the pillow and she saw the picture on his nightstand. The picture of Michele and Kevin and Stephanie and Michael. It had been his favorite. They'd been skiing at Michael's lodge. It had been such a happy time for all of them. Kevin hadn't died in a plane crash and Stephanie hadn't died in a car crash, leaving Michele and Michael to pick up the pieces and carry on. Michael was Kevin's twin brother.

Michele sat bolt upright and stared at the photo. His *identical* twin brother. *Ohmygod! Would he? Could they? Jeez, what an odd thought!*

She shook her head and ran her fingers through long auburn tresses that were tangled from tossing and turning.

Nah. It would never fly. He'd never agree. Still . . . .

She walked into the bathroom, turned on the shower, and stood in front of the mirror looking at her reflection.

Like anyone would want to lay on top of her and impregnate her. *Look at yourself,* she admonished. *Stringy hair, sunken cheeks, bags under your eyes, and a swollen, red nose from crying. Michael, don't you want to do it with me?* she mocked as she drew off her nightgown and tossed it to the floor. The body wasn't bad, it could still entice, but Lord, the face and hair needed some work! She stepped into the shower and turned the dial to make it as hot as she could stand. Her eyes focused on her hand and the finger where she still wore Kevin's ring. *And when was the last time she'd had a manicure?*

As she hung her head under the pulsing stream, she laughed. Michael would never want her. She wasn't his type. But still . . . there were other ways to get pregnant these days that had nothing to do with sex.

For Amanda, she would do it. She knew that she would do anything. Now, how to get Michael on board with this little plan? He'd loved his brother greatly; he had been devastated when Kevin had died. Maybe he'd do it for Kevin, if not for her . . . if not for Amanda.

Michele poured a third cup of coffee. Mandy would be home soon. It would be so much easier to do this while Mandy was out of the house. But in two hours, she hadn't been able to build up the courage. Just how did you call a brother-in-law who was half way across the country and ask for a teaspoon of his sperm?

Picking up the phone, she dialed Gabby's house and asked to speak to Amanda. It would not do for Amanda to come strolling in while she was talking to Michael about making a baby.

"Hi, babe. Did you sleep well last night?"

"Okay. I had to get up once to take some of my medicine, my head was hurting a little."

"Is it hurting now? Have you eaten anything yet?" Michele asked, the concern very apparent in her voice.

"No, Mom. I'm fine. And Gabby and I just finished some pancakes."

"When are you coming home? It's almost ten o'clock."

"Can I stay for another hour? Please?"

"Sure. And remember to thank Gabby's mom."

"Thanks, Mom. I will."

Well, that bought her an hour. No way would Amanda come home early. She never did. Both girls used every minute of their curfews, running through the front door with hardly a second to spare. It was wonderful that Amanda had such a good friend, especially now. But now, she had to worry about Gabby, too. This year was going to be a bitch for everybody.

She grabbed her coffee, warmed it in the microwave, and trudged up the stairs to her bedroom, just in case Amanda did come home early.

Michael lived in Denver. He was a surgeon, specializing in pediatrics. He lived in a gorgeous chalet set into a snowcapped mountain with Sam, his only child from his marriage to Stephanie. Sam was Amanda's age and as opposite as two cousins could possibly be.

The most remarkable thing about Sam, other than his impressive height, was his level of maturity. Every once in a while, you meet a very young child who knows without a doubt what he or she's going to be when they grow up. They never waiver, they never have a doubt. Sam was just that child. He knew from the age of five that he was going to be a doctor, and not just any kind of doctor. He knew he was going to be a vascular surgeon long before he should have been able to even pronounce it. So Sam was never a kid, never would be. He was born gifted, excelled at everything, and took nothing for granted. He was the kind of kid every parent dreamed about. Michele smiled as she remembered Sam opening his Christmas present one year. A deluxe microscope with trays and trays of extra slides. He'd been six then. Amanda hadn't even been able to read but he knew the Latin names for bugs—the viral kind.

She found Michael's number in her phone book and punched in the series of numbers. Then she listened to it ring, her nervousness making her underarms sticky. Usually, they communicated by e-mail. She hadn't actually talked to Michael for almost six months.

"Hello?"

"Michael?"

"Shelley?"

She smiled at his use of his nickname for her. "Yes. It's me."

"Well, how the hell are ya? Haven't talked to you in ages."

"I'm fine. It's Amanda who's in trouble. We got the reports back that we were waiting for. I e-mailed the results to you late last night."

"And?"

"It doesn't look good. They say she's probably not going to make it. The treatments didn't work," she sobbed on the last words.

"Oh, Shelley, I'm so sorry sweetheart. Please don't cry, you're tearin' me up here. What exactly are the numbers?"

"I sent them to you late last night, I knew you'd want to see them."

"And Dr. Corrish says there's no other avenue? Nothing else we can try?"

We. He'd said we. Maybe . . . just maybe . . . .

"There's nothing they can do, unless something else develops."

"How long are they talking?"

"A year, maybe a little more. It depends on how she handles the medicine and everything else."

"How are you holding up?"

"Michael, this is so hard. I can't even tell you."

"I can't even imagine."

"Michael?"

"Yes?"

"Are you busy right now?"

"No. I just got back from playing racquetball. I've got to go to the hospital for rounds, but I've got time. Talk to me."

"Michael, I want to ask you something. This is very hard for me, so give me some time to get it out and when I do, don't answer right away, okay? Think about it for a day or two and then call me back."

"Okay . . . ."

"Promise you'll think about it?"

"Shelley, what? What is it? Just ask me."

She took a deep breath and then just blurted it out. "I need to have a baby."

"What?"

"In order to save Amanda's life I need to have a baby. And it would be best if I had it with you."

"You're looking for an umbilical cord donor aren't you?"

"Yes."

"It doesn't always work you know, bone marrow is second only to the brain for its complexity."

"It's a chance and that's more than we have now."

"It's expensive, it's risky, and in some places it's illegal."

"Is that why you never mentioned it as a possibility?" Her voice was accusing right now.

He reacted to it, "No! I never mentioned it because there was no baby!"

"But there could be."

"It never occurred to me you'd want to conceive one just for this! With me no less!"

"You're the perfect candidate. You and Kevin were twins. The baby would have everything the same as Amanda. It would be a perfect match."

"That's not necessarily so. The same parents have vastly different kids all the time. That's why this procedure is so risky. No one ever knows if it's going to work or not."

"I understand we'd have to have some luck here."

"Yeah. Luck. Lots of it! One baby, one chance."

"I read something on-line where parents can conceive by in vitro fertilization, they can have many embryos to choose from and they can have them tested for tissue matching."

"Tissue typing for selective screening is against the law. Besides, we don't have enough time for that."

We don't have enough time for that.

She couldn't believe he'd said that. *We. We* don't have enough time for that. Her heart was beating so hard, she was sure he could hear it across the phone line.

The line was silent for a few moments. She didn't know what to say. Had he agreed?

She heard a big drawn out sigh and he answered the question for her, "Of course, I'll do it. If you're sure this is what you want to do, what choice do I have? Kevin would expect it of me."

"Oh Michael! Thank you! Thank you so much!"

"No problem. It's not that often that I get a call from a beautiful woman asking for a donation of that sort. I suppose you want me to collect it and overnight it. Although I could come to San Francisco and personally deposit it in the traditional manner if you'd prefer?"

She could see his quirky smile right over the phone line as he teased her.

And he could see her cheeks going crimson from the suggestion.

Ignoring his comment, she said, "I don't know when I need it. I need to check my cycle."

"You're going to need help with this. You're going to need to boost your hormones, and you might want to consider taking fertility pills."

"I'm very fertile. Kevin and I conceived Amanda the very first time we had unprotected sex."

"That's not what I mean. You may want to consider carrying more than one baby. Increasing the odds a little, so to speak."

"More than one baby!"

"Yeah. And if you had time for IVF I might be able to get some DNA testing done on the grounds that you need to screen for a particular genetic defect, then use the DNA gathered from all the embryos to select an egg to implant. Then we'd be sure you'd have a baby with the right match. But it doesn't sound like we have the time for that."

"More than one baby!"

"Yeah. You need to increase the odds that you'll have a tissue match. You want to have multiple embryos, only you won't cull any out like they do in the test tube. You carry them all. With IVF only four out of five implants take because the embryos don't stick to the lining of the uterus. The L-selectin protein on the embryo and the short-timed fertility secretion on the uterus lining have to be in exact synchrony or you don't get a baby. It's nearly impossible to time with IVF, but if your ovary releases the egg naturally, the uterus knows when to send the secretion. *Voila*, baby, or in this case babies."

"Michael, after this is over, I don't want six or seven children!"

"We never spoke about what was going to happen to the baby."

"I'll keep it of course! Why, I couldn't possibly do otherwise."

"Maybe if you had multiples, you could consider adoption. There's never a problem placing newborns."

"Oh, Michael, this is too much to think about. Can't we just have one?"

"Sweetheart, we can have as many as you like. You just let me know the day I have to do my part. I'll e-mail you the name of a specialist in San Francisco who can help you pinpoint your cycle and advise you on the fertility issue."

"Michael, thank you."

"It's the least I can do. Give Mandy a hug for me. Maybe Sam and I can get away for the baby shower," he joked.

"And just this morning I was thinking how good my body was still looking," she said ironically.

"Really?" his interest peaked.

"Not a stretch mark on it . . . yet. 'Bye, Michael. Love you."

"Love you, too."

Did he really just agree to sire who knows how many children? Good God, what a pickle. Damned if you do, damned if you don't. But there was no decision here. If the tables were turned, it would be the same. Kevin would do it for Sam, he knew that without a doubt.

He ran up the stairs to take a shower before heading out to the hospital. On his way, he knocked on Sam's door.

"Enter."

"Need a favor, Bud."

"Yeah? What's that?"

"Do some research on-line for me or at the library, if you'd rather. You can take my new Lexus. I need to know all the current research on umbilical cord uses, what's new in the world of fertility medication and fetal advance tissue typing. No, never mind the last one, she'd never abort, I'm almost sure of that. Use these key words to search: test tube embryos; embryo screening for tissue typing; social sex selection; designer babies; in vitro fertilization; spare parts from embryos; embryonic ethics. One resource might be the British Human Fertilization and Embryology Authority. I think they're the only ones pushing legislation on this kind of thing."

Sam was scribbling notes, trying to get everything down, but still he asked, "Care to tell me what this is all about?"

"Tonight. Remind me."

As if I'd forget, he said to himself as he stripped off his workout clothes and stepped into the room-sized shower.

As he drove his Mercedes coupe around the busy city streets, Michael thought about Stephanie and how she'd feel about all this. Stephanie had wanted to have more children, she just hadn't been sure it would have been the best thing for Sam. Many times she'd told him that a child like Sam needed more attention, more focus than ordinary children and she wasn't sure she could give him what he needed if their family grew. It was an issue they'd never really resolved before she ran off the road swerving to avoid an elk. She had died just two months after Kevin. He still came home sometimes, expecting to see her in the kitchen.

In the hospital parking lot, he forced himself to put aside his personal issues. His patients were paying top dollar, and even if they weren't, his patients, his "kids" would get his undivided attention. He loved his work and he was proud of the fact that he was one of the best in a field of many. It had never surprised him that Sam loved the world of medicine as much as he did, because he loved it so much himself.

The nurses at the station visibly straightened and checked their hair for stray wisps. He looked down at the first chart he was handed and smiled. You'd think after all this time, they'd know he was off limits. He hadn't even bothered to try to find a replacement for Stephanie, hadn't even dated. She had been "it" for him and he doubted that he'd ever find another woman to compare. He and Sam were fine all alone. They had their ski toys, they had their medicine, and they had their limitless stack of delivered pizzas. For men of medicine, they really didn't eat very well.

Ovulation

AN EGG IS RELEASED FROM AN OVARY INTO THE FALLOPIAN TUBE.

D r. Kay saw Michele two days later. He was an older man, probably conventional in his thinking, but decidedly the best in his field if the waiting room was any indication. He listened to her, but shushed her when she started talking about the pregnancy as it related to Amanda's disease.

"Don't need to know all that. I'm sure Michael is up on all that and has advised you. He said my job is to get you pregnant as fast as I can and to tell you he thinks you should go for triplets." He gave her a big grandfatherly smile and waited for her reaction.

"Of course, he'd say that," she smirked, "it's the same contribution on his part."

Dr. Kay laughed heartily as he handed her pamphlets to read, a basal thermometer, and two types of testing kits. He'd already asked her about her cycle, explained the mucus and ferning process, and determined their window was eleven days away. They needed to pinpoint it as accurately as possible. Michael would begin freezing and over-nighting his contributions in four days. Michele would begin taking special fertility hormones immediately.

Michael and Dr. Kay had already agreed on Pergonal instead of Clomid early this morning when Michael had called Dr. Kay at home. They wanted separate female gametes, each fertilized by a separate sperm so that they would end up with individual zygotes—these babies would not be identical if they could help it.

Dr. Kay wanted three specimens from Michael, just in case. Any heat would kill the sperm, and, as it was almost August, that could be crucial.

Michele went home to hide all the stuff she'd been given and to read everything both Michael and Sam had e-mailed her and now, all Dr. Kay's pamphlets too, before Amanda got home from summer school. She was making up classes she had missed last year because of her illness and Gabby, good friend that she was, accompanied her everyday.

"Mom says you can spend the night this Friday, if you want. She said she'd even take us shopping," Mandy said to Gabby as they walked down the hall to class. "She's been in a pretty good mood for the last few days. I've learned to take advantage of these good days. There's a few new CDs I'd like to get and there's this cool sweater at Pac Sun that would look so rad on me. What about you?"

"I need new shoes."

"You don't need new shoes."

"Yeah, yeah I do. Red is out—gray is in. I like the new Skechers at Foot Locker."

"Think your mom will spring for them?"

"I know I probably shouldn't say this, but I think we can both pretty much write our own ticket for a while. They're really worried about us."

"Yeah, but I don't want my mom broke when I'm gone."

"It's not like we're at the mall every day or beggin' to go to Disney World."

"We did that last year."

"Yeah, that was cool. We should go to Six Flags this year."

"I should choose, you get to choose next year."

The sobering thought caused them both to turn and stare at each other, the humor temporarily gone from their conversation.

"I don't care where we go Mandy, you pick. I just don't want to go to Alaska."

"I want to go to the Bahamas!"

"Great. When do we start working on them?"

"Right after Christmas. If we start talking about it before, we'll get less for Christmas."

"Good point."

The bell rang and they slipped into the room right in front of the teacher.

Michael and Sam sat at the breakfast table drinking orange juice and eating warmed-up pizza. They had both been up late on their respective computers doing research and compiling Michael's notes from colleagues all over the world.

Sam had not been thrilled to hear what his father was up to, but after thinking about it for a while, it all made sense to him. He could see why his father had agreed to do it. It was one of the things his father was so well known for . . . never giving up when it involved the life of a child.

Sam knew his father had just come from the front door and that he had handed a small package over to a Federal Express carrier.

"So, how'd you do it?"

They both knew what he was talking about, but Michael pretended he didn't.

Sam simply cocked one raised eyebrow at him, waiting for the answer. When none came, he persisted. "*Playboy, Penthouse, Hustler?* Or did you think of Mom?"

"No, I didn't think of Mom," he whispered harshly. "Nothing so tender and piquant would have done the trick, believe me. I needed something a bit more earthy, if you know what I mean."

Sam kept his eyebrow cocked, "Well?"

"If you must know, I thought about Betty Laughlin with the big boobs in the back seat of my '67 Chevelle."

Both of Sam's eyebrows went up then.

Then Michael tried to justify his naughty thoughts by saying, "I hadn't met your Mom yet."

There was silence for a few moments then he added, "Besides, I was just recalling memories, I'm allowed to do that."

Still silence.

"It doesn't matter anyway. It worked and that's all I care about."

"When will we know?"

"In a few weeks."

Michele finished the dinner dishes and then helped Mandy with a homework project. While Mandy was taking a shower, she walked into her office and booted up her computer. The first message in the Inbox of her e-mail account was from Michael. She clicked on it to open it. There was only one short line so she leaned over the chair to read it before sitting down.

`Was it as good for you as it was for me?`

She smiled and was surprised by how good it felt to smile again. She pulled out the chair and sat down. Her fingers flew over the keys.

`At least you had human contact. I had a cold syringe with an even colder injection. I think it might still have been frozen, I sure didn't feel anything swimming up there. I get to do it again tomorrow. If you really enjoyed your part, have at it! Love Shelley.`

Mandy stood in the doorway toweling her hair, "Whatcha doin', Mom?" she had a puzzled expression on her face.

"Just answering an e-mail. Why the funny look? You've seen me do this hundreds of times."

"Yeah, but I don't ever remember seeing you smile while you were doing it."

Michele spun around in her chair, put her cupped hands on her knees, and looked intently at Mandy. "Well, get used to it kiddo, there's going to be a whole lot more smilin' goin' on around here from now on!"

"Why? What's going on?"

"I can't tell you yet. It's a secret. But I think I may have things all worked out."

A wary look crossed Mandy's face. "Not another doctor! Please, I don't want to see another doctor!"

Michele stood up and walked over to Mandy. She wrapped her arms around her terry-clad daughter and inhaled the sweet peaches and cream fragrance lingering from her shower. She hugged her tightly and softly rocked her back and forth.

"No, baby. No more new doctors. At least not for a while."

"Then what is it?"

"I can't tell you now, it may not pan out. But soon. Soon, everything will work out. You'll see. Now go dry that hair, I don't want you catching a cold."

"Motherrrr. You know you can't get a cold from wet hair."

"Humor me. It's something I've believed all my life. I'm not going to throw caution to the wind now, especially when any bug you get could land you back in the hospital. Now go use your blow dryer and dry it. Please."

"Yes, Mother," Mandy said condescendingly.

While Mandy went to her room, Michele went back to her computer. She paid a few bills and then just for fun, visited a few web sites that sold nursery items. She honestly didn't have a feeling one way or the other as to whether she was pregnant right now or not, but since it was a possibility, as it hadn't been for many, many years, she reveled in the uncertainty of it. There was an innate excitement in her, a feeling of revival instead of the deep down depression that she'd lived with for so long.

Just before sliding into her bed and turning off her bedside lamp, she tried to conjure up the image of Michael as she remembered him. As she slid between the crisp linens, she wondered if he'd changed a lot since the last time she'd seen him and she wondered for a moment or two if he'd be truly happy if she was carrying his baby right now.

Conception

THE EGG HAS BEEN FERTILIZED BY THE SPERM; THE OVUM DIVIDES.

r. Kay wanted only a slight overlapping of exposure for conception, and since Michele's first semen injection had been at ten the day before, he wanted to see her at two o'clock today. Twenty-four to thirty hours being the average time that sperm could live in a warm vagina. So Michele had arranged to have a facial, a manicure and pedicure, and her hair done at the salon across the street from the doctor's office. For some reason she wanted to be close to the place where part of her future child's genetic makeup was. It was a ridiculous feeling, she knew. But she just had to be close to the other part that would make her whole again.

Maybe it was the idea that she could be close to Kevin this way. Michael was so like him, his sperm would be comprised of exactly the same things that Kevin's had been when it had swam inside her. Maybe she was just losing it.

As the woman standing above her spread one cream after another on her face, Michele sank further in the chair, unconsciously angling her feet higher in the recliner willing Michael's essence of life to find a haven. One, two, or three perfect little eggs that would make Mandy some brothers or sisters. She really didn't care how many now, just so long as one had what it took to make Mandy well.

"You look quite different than you did yesterday," Dr. Kay said as he sat at his desk across from her.

"Yes, I took the time to have some badly needed grooming done. I've been neglectful lately. But now that I'm having quasi-sex every day, I thought I should take some extra care and dress for the occasion. Wouldn't want the new kids to be disappointed with their new mama."

Dr. Kay chuckled. "Somehow, I don't think they will be. One more round tomorrow and then in a few weeks we'll draw some blood and see what we have. Remember, no bath again tonight."

"Don't worry, Doctor, I'm not about to flush out the father."

He took her into the examining room and gave her another injection of Michael's sperm. Then he left her to wait, flat on her back with her knees bent and her hips tilted back. For twenty minutes she laid there reading Leonard Nilsart's book describing what the sperm were supposed to be doing at this precise moment. She read the text out loud to encourage the fresh batch of sperm inside her to swim hard and be conquering.

Then Dr. Kay came back in and helped her off the table.

"Good. See you tomorrow then, and do try to relax. That's really the most helpful thing you can do right now."

"Easy for you to say," she said as he held the door for her. To herself she added, *There's so much riding on this.*

Gabby looked over at Mandy as they sat in the cafeteria eating wilted salads with brown-tinged fruit.

"What did you say you needed my help with the other day?"

Mandy let out a long sigh and then quickly let the words spill out, "I don't want my mom to be all alone when I'm gone. I want you to help me find her a new husband."

"Really?" Gabby asked. Not convinced that this was actually a serious conversation, she mimicked her favorite actress, Alicia Silverstone from *Clueless.* She even let her hand flop from her wrist in the engaging way that Alicia had.

"Yeah. I want her to fall in love again. To have something to live for after I'm gone."

When Gabby realized that Mandy hadn't picked up on her sarcasm, she deadpanned, "And just how do we do this?"

"I've got a few ideas, but I'll need your help. Are you in?"

Shifting in her seat, she shrugged her shoulders. "Sure, I'll do what I gotta do if it'll make you happy."

"It will make me very happy if we can pull this off without her finding out."

"Well, when do we start?"

"Today, after school. The only problem, is that I need a computer and Mom is always on ours."

"Tell her you have some homework you need to do. She always gets off when you tell her that."

"Yeah, that'll work."

"So what are we going to do on the computer?"

"We're going to go on-line to a dating service."

"Don't we have to have her permission to do that?"

"Duh! Of course we do. That's why we're doing it all over the computer. We're gonna be her. The dating service will never know that it's not her they're dealing with."

"And just how are we going to manage that?"

"Simple. I know everything there is to know about her. I can scan one of her pictures over to them. I can set up a password account to receive messages so Mom doesn't find out."

"What about paying them? What are you going to do about that?"

"Yeah, there's always a catch."

Then Mandy thought for a minute. "Well, no, not really. We can work around it. Mom's accounts are all on the computer. I can get her charge card number and charge it."

"And she'll find out as soon as she gets her statement."

"Maybe, maybe not. I can get the address from the statement and send a change of address to them. Then the next bill will go to . . . say, a post office box. We get the bill, we pay it, and all's clear. See?"

"It's just not going to work that smoothly and you know it. What happens when she misses the bill? And I didn't know you had that kind of money."

"She'll call and ask for another. Don't you see? It'll buy us the time we need. And I only have to pay the minimum on the card balance, not the whole thing. Eventually, she's going to find out. She has to! She has to go on some of these dates! And if it works out the way I think it will, she'll be happy to pay the rest of the charges."

"So, we tell her then? Just before springing it on her that her date is picking her up for dinner? Oh, and by the way, we used your charge card," Gabby mimicked Alicia again.

"It won't come down that way. Trust me. We have plenty of time to figure all that out. First, we have to get started. We have to get her picture and profile on-line so men can see it and choose her."

"Are you going to use an old picture? Because she really hasn't been looking all that . . ." What was a word she could say that wouldn't make Mandy mad? " . . . all that . . . dateable."

"Yes, I know. She needs a little work. We're going to have to take care of that, too. She just needs some sleep and a little something done to her hair. It's gotten long and stringy. She's just been putting it in a ponytail. It's lifeless. I've been telling her that for months. It needs something, some color or streaks, maybe even layering."

"Okay, so we get her dolled up, we get her on-line, she gets picked, then what?"

"Then we have to tell her. But not until the guy's out of his car and heading for the door."

"Oh, she's just gonna love this!" Gabby said sarcastically.

Mandy smiled, "Yeah, I know," she said sheepishly. "But the idea is for her to love somebody else and this is the best thing I could come up with."

"So, we go with it. As soon as we get home, you tell her you need the computer for homework. I'll be your lookout."

"Good plan. Are you actually eating that mushy pear?" Mandy asked, grimacing.

"Yeah. I'm pretending it's Gerber's strained pears. You know how much I still love them."

"You and your baby food," Mandy said as she stood up and gathered the trash in one hand and her books in the other. "Are you still eating that banana pudding stuff, too?"

"Yeah, it's good stuff and don't make faces at me, you're the one who got me started on it last year when it was all you could eat."

"You're a good friend. How many other girls can boast that their best friend gave up soda and pizza for six months to have sleepovers that consisted of nothing but tapioca pudding and strained carrots?"

"You were suffering. I wanted to be a part of it for you. But it was the all night puking that really tested our friendship. I just couldn't do that for you. Hell, I had a hard time just listening to it."

"I know. And I appreciate it, Gabby. There's never been a better friend than you."

"Yeah, well, when your mother comes down on us for this next escapade, don't be surprised if I'm not standing behind you anymore."

"It would probably be better if you weren't. She'd never be mad at me. I'm too sick. That's why this is going to work. She won't want to upset me, so she'll go along with it. I'm almost sure of it."

"Okay, if you say so. See ya after school."

The bell rang and they headed down different hallways. Gabby shook her head at the things she let Mandy talk her into, and Mandy shook her head at Gabby's lack of faith in her perfect plan.

When Mandy and Gabby got home that afternoon, they were shocked to see the transformation in Mandy's mom. Speechless, they both walked around her admiring her new hair style and the new way she was wearing makeup.

"Mom, you look terrific! When did you do all this?" Mandy asked, gesturing with her hand from her mother's new, soft copper tresses, down to the floor where she stood barefoot showing off her shiny crimson toenails.

Michele smiled at what she assumed was praise. "I treated myself this morning. Your mother was beginning to look like a haggard old witch, so I decided to spruce up a bit."

"I'll say," Gabby said, then quickly covered her mouth with her hand as she realized what she'd just said. "Sorry, Mrs. M. I didn't mean . . . ."

"I understand Gabby, don't worry about it. I know I was getting pretty rough around the edges. But now," she said as she flipped her hair up off her neck with her hand, "I'm a new woman."

"Yeah. You're beautiful again," Mandy whispered. There was no mistaking the wistfulness in her voice and it brought tears to Michele's eyes.

She pulled Mandy close and hugged her. "I'm sorry I let myself go for so long, I just couldn't think of anything but you and getting you better."

"So what's changed?" Mandy asked suspiciously.

Michele smiled broadly and took both girls by the shoulders as she led them over to a kitchen counter that was piled high with bakery boxes.

"Still too soon to tell, but soon. Pretty soon, we'll have some good news on this home front. Now help me open these boxes, I know there's a cheesecake in one of these. And for you

Gabby," she said as she dramatically pulled a donut box out of a bag, "Krispy Kremes, piping hot!"

"Ooh!" Gabby sighed and she practically drooled as she reached for them. "Thank you."

"Don't eat more than half the box okay? Otherwise your mother's going to kill me!"

Mandy found the box with the strawberry cheesecake and the three of them sat at the kitchen table wolfing down the sugary confections like they were their last meal.

"Can I guess at the good news?" Mandy mumbled over a mouthful of cheesecake.

"Don't talk with your mouth full. And no, you may not guess, because first of all you'll never guess, not in a million years, and second, even if you did, I wouldn't tell."

"When then?"

Michele glanced up at the calendar on the wall and mentally counted off the days. "By next Wednesday I should be ready to spill the beans."

"Did you win the lottery?"

"No guessing, but no, I didn't win the lottery."

"Find a job like you used to have with the gallery?"

"No, I didn't find a job. I'm not even looking. My job is taking care of you. Now stop guessing."

"An old college classmate looked you up and he's yummy," Gabby joined in, getting into the game.

"Gabby," Michele chided, but she smiled broadly at her. "Not hardly. You'll never guess, you might as well just wait until next week."

"You bought me a pony?" Mandy said gleefully.

"No."

"A puppy?"

"No."

"A goldfish?"

"You want a goldfish?"

"No, although I wouldn't mind a puppy," Mandy added.

"No puppies. No pets. At least not now. Not when we never know when we're going to have to spend weeks in the hospital."

"That means never then!" Mandy said defiantly.

"I don't know about that. I have a hunch you're going to get better."

"That's the secret, isn't it? You've found something. Some miracle elixir."

"Possibly. But that's all I'm saying for now," Michele said as she grabbed a donut from the box in front of Gabby and stuffed the whole thing into her mouth.

Both girls laughed as Michele tried to chew it without any of it coming out of her mouth.

"Now Mom, you always tell me to take small bites."

She smiled over at her daughter and ran a finger down her cheek. "Yes, I do. And you remember that with steak. I don't think it much matters with Krispy Kreme donuts, they melt. Now, go get your homework done."

"I need the computer," Mandy said as she stole a glance over at Gabby.

"Okay, it's already booted up. Just make sure you don't jam the printer again, okay?"

"Okay," Mandy said as she stood and picked up her book bag from the floor. "C'mon Gabby, looks like the hard part of our homework is done."

"What's that mean?" Michele asked.

"Nothing. Just that stage one on our project is pretty much already together."

Both girls giggled as they climbed the stairs. Michele shook her head at the two silly girls as she wiped down the table. The girls had known each other since they were five and it was not at all unusual for them to speak in riddles that she couldn't understand. Teenagers! What were they up to now?

"Boy, after loading in all this information, I can't believe that now they want me to take a test."

"Yeah, and a test that you have to answer the way your Mom would."

"How hard can it be? I think I know her preeettty well. I know all there is to know about her. Here goes." Mandy clicked the icon to start the on-line test that the dating service was requiring; some kind of thing they were using to determine someone's character.

"Numero uno. 'Which flowers make the best romantic gift? A. Red roses, B. Unusual and exotic tropical flowers, C. Wildflowers, D. Potted, flowering plants, E. I don't think flowers are a good romantic gift.' Well, Dad used to send her white roses when he was away, so red is out. She keeps killing all the Bonsai trees I give her for Mother's Day, so exotic tropical is out. We have lots of wildflowers out back she could pick anytime, so I don't think she'd appreciate them. And all our potted, flowering plants are silk. How do you think I should answer this, Gab?"

"I thought you knew all there was to know about her, huh?"

"Not in the romantic sense, apparently. Which one should I click on?"

"Wildflowers. At least you know she likes them. And they're cheap so it won't make anyone think she's high maintenance."

"Good point." She clicked on 'C.'

"Next. 'If a woman makes more money than her husband, how do you think it will affect the relationship? A. The husband will become resentful, B. They'll fight more about money, C. They'll fight more about money than if the man was the breadwinner, D. It will not have a negative effect on their relationship.' I don't think money's ever been a big issue with Mom, there's always been enough, and even when she was working, Dad could have cared less about her paycheck. I remember sometimes they had to call her to tell her to come pick it up whenever she sold a painting. So, I vote for D. How 'bout you?"

"Yeah. She wouldn't care how much he made. Hell, she's not making any now, so it would be hard for him to make less."

"Good point." She clicked on 'D.'

"'If your partner started yelling at you during a disagreement, how would you respond? A. I'd do whatever I could to decrease the tension, B. I'd yell back, C. I'd calmly ask my partner to fully explain how he or she is feeling.' That's a tough one. I know it wouldn't be B. She'd never yell back."

"Yeah, I don't think I've ever heard your mom really yelling. Not like my mom, anyway."

"I think I'll go with 'A,' because I seem to remember one time when they were upset about something, Mom rubbed Daddy's back until he calmed down."

Gabby was looking over Mandy's shoulder. "Only two more to go." She read one out loud over Mandy's shoulder, "'You find a nice watch on an empty table in a restaurant. Would you keep it?'"

"Nah. I know she wouldn't. She doesn't even wear a watch half the time."

"Hey, that was funny, 'half the time,'" Gabby chuckled. "You're right, she'd never keep it. Remember that time at the shoe store when they gave her too much change? She actually walked back in and gave it back to them."

"Yeah, she's like that. Next?"

"'If a male friend of yours decided to be a stay-at-home dad while his wife worked, what would your reaction be?'"

"She'd say go for it. She thinks men don't do enough with their kids as it is."

"We're done," Gabby said. "Click on submit and let's see who's compatible."

"We won't know today, Gabby. It takes a few days for them to process everything. Then if someone wants to contact her, they do it by e-mail."

"What if she checks her e-mail?"

"I used my e-mail account. It'll come to me."

"Good thinking."

"Yeah, I've thought this out well. Wouldn't surprise me a bit if Mom's not madly in love with her perfect soul mate in less than a month or two."

"Cool. Now let's get the real homework done."

"Get me that history web site Mrs. Graham gave us to check out. Might as well get that report started first."

They worked quietly until dinnertime and then Gabby left to go home, giving Mandy a secret smile when Mandy's mom asked if they were finished with the computer for the evening.

It was dark outside and it seemed to Mandy that the rest of the world was asleep. Everyone was down and out, except for her. As Mandy strolled around her dimly-lit room, she picked up the odd knick-knack here and there, remembering the special occasion that attached her to it: the little Precious Moments statuette that Gabby had given her on their Confirmation Day; the raggedy softball that she and her dad had tossed back and forth so many times that the cover was peeling back; the stack of photo albums showcasing the special times of her life. Was her life soon to be over? Was that last album on the far bookcase hutch, the one with only a handful of pages filled, was that to be the final chronicle of her existence here on earth? Would that be so bad, she wondered.

When her dad had died, she had spent months trying to figure out a way to go with him; trying to find a way to cross over to him. She'd been terrified thinking that he was all alone on the other side of the universe, in a place she thought of as pitch black and cold. She'd only been nine then and hadn't understood the absolute permanency of death, and thought that maybe she could just go for a visit. But with her illness had come the acceptance of the idea that death was permanent. An irrevocable isolation from everything she now knew for an existence debated around the globe as nirvana, at best, or eternal black nothingness, at worst.

If she hadn't discovered that death held no more than a dismal promise from the many teary-eyed chats with kids in similar straits, she would've gleaned it from the reactions of the parents to their children's bleak futures, her mom's included.

Oh sure, parents spouted scripture and made everything seem so ethereally blissful, but it wasn't as if anybody was happily sending their child off to Camp Heaven, now was it? The way her mom was so adamant that Mandy not go that direction, no matter what, made Mandy know, without a doubt, that death was a hole you could never dig out of. A hole where no one ever visited, where there was no pizza, no Mary Kate & Ashley movies and no anticipated Christmas mornings of glittering trees and presents piled higher than she stood. She walked over to her window and looked out on the trim, square yard fifteen feet below.

A few feet out from her window was a big live oak tree. It was missing a limb about four feet up from where the roots wove in and out of patchy, uneven grass, and over the years, the bark had grown around the wound where the limb had been severed, making what appeared to be a small door with a rounded arch at the top. When she was little, she used to knock on the little door, asking the witch who she knew lived inside, to open the door and come out to play. Everyday she knocked on the door and talked to the imaginary crone that she believed lived inside, asking her to be her playmate. And then one day, a moving van pulled up to the curb not ten feet from where she stood knocking on the smooth wood. She watched as the movers unloaded boxes of toys and miniature-sized white and gold furniture. Then a station wagon pulled in behind the van and Gabby had run out of one of the back doors. They had been inseparable ever since. And every once in a while, when Gabby did something Mandy didn't particularly like, she'd bend over and whisper softly in her ear, "Little witch." The significance was lost on Gabby as she thought Mandy was simply too straight-laced to use the word "bitch."

Mandy's head ached as it often did at night, but she wasn't tired enough to lay down and obliterate the headache with sleep. Instead, she reached for her notebook and propped herself up in bed. She'd write a poem. With flourishes equal to that of an accomplished calligrapher, she penned words that would one day, in her mind, make her a revered poet laureate. Words that she knew didn't come just from her soul, but from that of her father's lingering one.

Knock, knock, who's not there?
Something tells me you don't care.
Read the names—acknowledge none,
Nothing lost to you, you're done.

Catch a glimpse of many lines,
Who deserves the *New York Times*?
Earn yourself a better name,
So you can leave a page of shame.

Richard Kane—two sentence man
Died last night while in a jam.
Money, none. Fame—oh no,
Goodbye to you—one line, whoa!

Mr. Fleishman, treasury official
Duty calls, three line ritual.
What is said is what you've done,
To hell with you, I'd give you one.

One does wonder what he'll do,
When he goes, lines one or two?

Heroes deserve a front page spread,
God, don't let me die in bed!

She titled it "Obituary Column." Then she closed her notebook, stuck the pencil in the spiral wire on the side, and tucked the journal into her nightstand drawer. Maybe now she was a little tired. Her head ached and her bones felt achy and soft. She tugged lightly on a wisp of hair by her ear and smiled when it didn't come out. Even if she was getting sicker because her treatments had stopped, her hair was growing in. It appeared it would be curlier than it had been and maybe even a little thicker. Although she was sure that was just wishful thinking on her part.

2 Weeks

THE OVUM DIVIDES AND REDIVIDES RAPIDLY, FORMING A CLUSTER
OF CELLS.

Four pregnancy tests couldn't be wrong. She knew she didn't need the blood test Dr. Kay was insisting on to know that she was pregnant. Inside her a new life was already growing. Cells splitting and dividing, blood building up to succor and caress a seedling. But how many? Could there possibly be two? Twins. That would be awesome, she thought. Her broad smile grinned back at her from the mirror over the bathroom sink. A baby, she thought as she gently rubbed her lower belly. A tiny, little baby.

She walked into her bedroom and reached for the phone, then she dialed Michael's office number. His secretary took her call and forwarded it to the floor where Michael was doing his rounds.

"Michael?"

"Shelley?"

"Mmhmm. Guess what?"

"Am I good or what?" he exclaimed, and you could hear the pride in his voice.

"Well you're certainly fast."

"Hey, don't let that get around all right? It would ruin my reputation."

"Yeah, right. Your reputation for what? I bet you haven't even had a date in all this time."

"Oh yeah, well this just goes to show you that the dating process is not all it's cracked up to be. Look at us, a few words on the telephone, a fast jet, and *voila* . . . procreation. Who needs to stammer over drinks and fork over big bucks for oysters on the half shell? So has it been verified by a blood test?"

"What is it with you doctors? Why don't you guys trust these over-the-counter kits? It says on the box that they're accurate and reliable."

"We don't believe any tests unless we order them ourselves. And, the blood test is much more specific when it comes to determining the amount of HCG or Human Chorionic Gonadotropin, which is a hormone the developing placenta secretes. Go get your blood tested and then call me back."

"Then I'm going to take Amanda out to dinner and tell her the good news!"

"Oh no! No, no, no! Don't do that!"

"Why not?"

"For a few reasons. Trust me on this. One, what if something happens? You could be setting her up for a real big let down. Remember, this will mean more to her than just a little brother or sister waiting in the wings. Wait a while, settle into it, and make sure everything's going along all right before you tell her. She has a lot at stake here, and you don't want to give her false hope."

"That makes sense. And two?"

"Two, time flies by so much slower when you're her age. Don't you remember how long your freshmen and sophomore years were?"

"Yeah. Forever."

"Don't make her wait for what will seem like an eternity to her."

"Is there a three?"

"Yes. Three, you have no idea how she's going to handle this news; she's been an only child all her life. You adjust to the idea first, then you'll be more prepared if she isn't exactly thrilled about all this. Which I guarantee you, she probably won't be, at first. And, you'll have more explaining to do than most mothers will. She's going to want to know how this happened. This isn't just birds and bees stuff anymore, you know."

"Good point. Okay, I'm on my way to have the test done. I'll call you when I get the results."

"Okay. And Shelley?"

"Yes?"

"Congratulations, sweetheart."

"Thanks."

The next afternoon she went to the doctor's office to get the results. Dr. Kay beamed, his round face and bald head reminding her of a grinning man on the moon. She called Michael as soon as she got home but was unable to talk directly to him, so she opted to e-mail him:

```
    Michael, your secretary said you're doing
an emergency surgery and that it could be
hours before you return my call. I just wanted
you to know that the blood test was positive.
Dr. Kay gave me some prenatal vitamins and
warned me off alcohol and coffee. Not too
much of a problem for me, except I have to
switch to decaffeinated teas now. He said he
could see me until the fourth month and then
I have to get a specialist since his field is
primarily in fertility issues. Somewhere in
```

```
the second or third month we'll find out if
it's one or two. Michele.
```

It wasn't until the next day that Michael chanced to check his e-mail. He thought that since he hadn't heard from Michele the day before, that she'd had bad news, namely that the blood test was negative, and that she was too disappointed to bother to call him back. It happened all the time with those home test kits. They were a good tool, but they really weren't as accurate as they were made out to be unless the woman was a bit farther along.

He clicked to open the letter and quickly scanned it. So, she really was pregnant. He had a child growing in a woman who was over a thousand miles away. It was an unnerving feeling. Sort of like being told you had a birthday cake, only all you got to see of it was a picture. It was a hollow joy. Nice to think about, but not really yours to get all worked up about. Except that he was worked up about it. Sure, there was a sense of pride—he'd done his duty and apparently, rather well. But there was more. A strange sort of possessiveness that was totally inappropriate. Or was it?

He drained his second cup of coffee and went to get ready for work. On his way to his bedroom he decided he'd switch to decaffeinated coffee. There would be a sort of cohesiveness linking them, he thought, if he gave up caffeine too. How hard could it be? And really, he should of done it years ago, anyway.

The first patient he saw on his rounds was the little boy he'd operated on the day before. He'd been hit by a car and had some serious shoulder and head trauma. He was fine now, barring infection; Michael had relieved the pressure on his skull just in time. He was being kept sedated to allow for the swelling and the pain to subside. His mother was sitting in a chair by his side when Michael entered the room. He mutely nodded to her as he made his way to the bed to examine her son. His total focus was on the boy in the bed in front of him until he chanced to glance over at the boy's mother and really look at her.

She was holding a tiny baby in her arms, holding it tightly to her chest as it nursed on her exposed breast. As a doctor this was not an unusual sight to see, especially in a hospital, just steps away from the maternity ward. But this time, he saw the common, everyday act of a mother feeding her child a little differently. His thoughts automatically went to Michele and he tried to envision her sitting there like that. A baby hugged to her, sucking and pulling on her dusky nipple.

The thought chased around in his mind that Michele was going to be nursing his kid like that. *His kid . . . or kids.* His baby would be sucking on her nipples, drawing life-sustaining essences out of her. Like I want to. *Good God, where had that come from?* He quickly turned away from the woman and looked back down at her son's chart.

But one thing occurred to him and that one thing was bothering him immensely. *Would she be doing it so openly, so any man could see, as this woman was?* A flash of unaccountable jealousy raged through him for a fleeting moment and he had to check himself. What the hell was going on? He had no right to be jealous of Michele's breasts. Hell, he didn't even have any control over whether Michele would nurse or not. Although as a pediatrician, he would certainly enumerate all the reasons that she should. As a man, well . . . as a man, the woman and her mystical breasts were giving him a hard-on three states over.

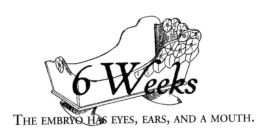

6 Weeks

THE EMBRYO HAS EYES, EARS, AND A MOUTH.

Michele managed to keep her pregnancy to herself. With the exception of Michael, she told no one—although it was very hard not to spill the beans when she talked to her mother who was on an eighty-day cruise in the Mediterranean. Her mother had been talked into taking this cruise by her best friend, who like herself had been widowed ten years earlier. It had been touted as an older singles' cruise and both women had their hearts set on finding the next man in their life somewhere on the Riviera, or better yet, in the gaming casinos of Monaco. They hadn't quite learned the harsh fact of life, that men in their fifties or sixties, especially men with money, tended to find companionship with women in their twenties. She decided to wait until her mother docked in Ensenada to let her know about her pregnant thirty-eight-year-old daughter. By then, she supposed, she would know how many babies she was going to be birthing.

When she felt she just had to talk to someone about it, Michele e-mailed Michael. He was a constant source of encouragement and always managed to sign off with some hilarious

comment regarding toughening her nipples for nursing, reminding her not to get a perm, or recommending a certain cocoa
butter cream for stretch marks. She felt a little guilty keeping
her prenatal vitamins hidden in her bathroom under the sink
and sneaking extra glasses of milk and slices of cheese while
Mandy was at school. At night, she took a bowl of ice cream up
to her room to eat while Mandy was showering. She waited
until Mandy went to school before trying to force down a
healthy breakfast, since typically lunch was her first meal of
the day.

There was only one thing that could have given her away
and that was if Mandy had cared to look at the new stacks of
reading material piling up on Michele's nightstand. Not an avid
reader herself, Mandy hardly seemed to notice or care what
other people were reading.

Meanwhile, both Sam and Michael were continually sending her articles to read, web sites to look up, and occasionally,
a hilarious cartoon.

9 Weeks

THE EYELIDS HAVE FORMED AND CLOSED OVER THE EYES.

Keeping such a big secret from Mandy was hard. Thank God she didn't have any morning sickness. But still, there were so many times when they were together that Michele thought of the baby. And many times she wanted to share the overwhelmingly good news with Mandy. But remembering Michael's words, she refrained. The end of the third month, when she was going into her second trimester, would be plenty soon enough. Then she could walk into all the baby departments she wanted to, accept baby literature mailed to the house, and hum lullabies out loud instead of to herself.

She'd had to make up something when the girls finally remembered that she'd had a secret to tell them. Coming up with the idea to give one of the guest rooms a total makeover did not seem to them to be the thrilling news that she had alluded to a few weeks earlier. How was that going to help anything? They just shook their head at her eccentricities and went off to complain about adults and their addlepated thoughts. Meanwhile, Michele planned a nursery on a baby web site for the new "guests."

The next day, Michele sat down to pay her bills and discovered she was missing a statement for one of her charge cards. When she called the charge card company and discovered that according to them, she had mailed a change of address card, she quickly had them research the most recent charges. Upon discovering that there was an on-line charge for $435.00 to a dating service called WEBDATE, she cringed. Oh dear God. Mandy had mentioned once that no boy would ever be interested in her with her "chemo hair" and her "bag-of-bones skin," but she never thought that Mandy would go on-line to try to find a boyfriend!

The more she thought about it though, the more she realized that maybe it wouldn't be so bad if she could find someone on-line to talk to, and maybe even eventually meet some boy who might get to know her first before being turned off by her illness.

Not usually a skeptic, but priding herself on keeping current, Michele knew a lot about the types of people who used on-line chat rooms and services. For the most part, they were lonely people reaching out for attention. Mandy certainly qualified on that score. But she was sure her daughter was not aware that under the guise of anonymity, people dissembled. The whole come-on for most people was that "anything goes, and no one knows."

How could she warn Mandy without tipping her off to what she knew? She decided to keep an eye on this WEBDATE site and what Mandy was up to on it. The last thing she needed was for her low-self-esteemed daughter to get hooked up with a sexual deviant trying to use her for money or for laughs. She knew Mandy's password, so she clicked over and signed on. That was funny. None of the passwords worked. Damn, she must have recently changed them. Now she'd have to wait her out and sneak up on her to find out what she was up to. And just what her $435.00 was buying. But why change the billing address on the charge card? Ah, of course. Mandy didn't want her to find out about the charge. Well, didn't she think she would eventually? This was a whole other matter. Amanda needed to be called down for this. God, how she hated to punish her when she was so sick.

Using her own password she went to the WEBDATE site and tried to find Amanda's profile in their free sampling section. She put in a myriad of search words trying to bring up her bio, but had no success. Maybe Amanda had become one of the new breed of Internet liars and was now a voluptuous SWF in search of a brawny SWM. Without knowing how Amanda would alter her personality and looks, Michele realized that she could search profiles forever—and of course, without joining, she didn't have access to all of them anyway. She clicked back to her bank's bill payer site and finished with her bills just in time to hear the school bus brakes screech at the bus stop two blocks away. *Well, well, well, Mutt & Jeff are home,* Michele thought. Should she press them and go for some answers now, or should she let them get at the brownies she'd baked this morning first?

Her good-natured side won through and she went downstairs to meet them. She was waiting on the front porch, the plate of brownies in her lap while she sat in a rocking chair, a tray of glasses filled with milk sitting on the top step.

The girls were chattering excitedly about something that had happened on the bus as they walked up the steps to greet her. The sight of the brownies made them both drop their book bags and plop down onto the steps. They talked about everything that had happened at school that day: the awful test in English; the boy who had tripped down the auditorium stairs on his way back to his seat; and the new girl from Scotland who had hair the color of rust and more freckles than you could ever count.

Then they hopped up to use the computer to do their homework. Michele thought about saying something about Internet dating or chat rooms, but decided against it. These days, a sneaky mom could do a lot more prudent prying by letting her fingers do the walking on the keyboard than by running into brick wall after brick wall from inane conversations. She'd find a way to access those files or figure out Mandy's new password. It was just a matter of time; she could be patient.

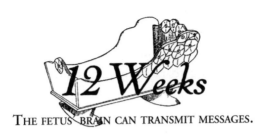

12 Weeks

THE FETUS BRAIN CAN TRANSMIT MESSAGES.

We got an answer! A guy on the web picked Mom to be his blind date this Saturday! His name is Milo Markovitch. He's part owner of the NAPA service shop on Mercantile. He's five foot seven, two hundred and five pounds and has his own horse and biplane!"

"Wow, that sounds so cool! How old is he? Is there a picture?"

"Yeah, hold on, I'm downloading it now."

Together the girls watched as the screen filled up with the image of a man who looked decidedly Greek in appearance. He had a rather large mustache and a prominent nose and lots of curly dark hair springing out all over his head.

"Not bad," Gabby said, as his chin filled in. "He doesn't look too old."

"He's got good teeth," Mandy added, pointing to his broad smile. "I bet he smiles a lot, that's good."

"What's it say down there?" Gabby asked, pointing to the white box under his picture.

"Hi, Michele. When I saw your picture I knew that we had to meet. It seems that we're interested in a lot of the same things. How about I pick you up next Saturday night and take you out to dinner? I know this nice place where we can really get to know each other over a bottle of wine. Your picture looks really bitchin'. I can't wait to see if you're really this pretty in person."

"That sounds nice."

"Yeah, it does, doesn't it? Except for the bitchin' thing. But Mom will straighten him out about his cussin'."

"Now, how do we pull this part of it off?"

"First," Mandy said, clicking on the keys, "we reply, 'Yes, I'd love to have dinner with you, your picture looks good too.' Then we worry about the rest on Saturday when he shows up."

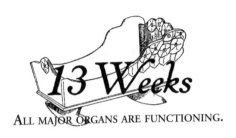

13 Weeks

ALL MAJOR ORGANS ARE FUNCTIONING.

She really didn't know why she was so excited. When Michael had called yesterday to say that he and Sam were coming to visit over the weekend, she had simply said, "That's nice. Mandy will love seeing Sam again. It's been quite a while since they've seen each other."

When Michael had teasingly asked, What about her, would she be happy to see him again?, she'd felt a strange quiver of anticipation race through her. But she had responded nonchalantly that, "Yes, yes, of course I'll be delighted to see you again. I can't wait."

They had talked for a few more minutes and decided that maybe Saturday night might be a good time to tell Mandy about the baby. Michael suggested that they tell Amanda together.

Michele was secretly relieved and grateful that she wouldn't have to be the one to broach all this with Mandy on her own. Michael always had such a calm manner and such a direct way of speaking. The more she thought about it, the more she was reassured about their visit.

She decided not to tell Mandy about Michael and Sam's visit in advance for two reasons: one, she knew that because of Michael's job, plans often had to be changed at the last minute; and two, the element of planning a nice surprise was an enticing one. She'd make a big pot of spaghetti sauce—the special family recipe—an antipasto salad with the zesty garlic dressing that Kevin and Michael used to prepare with such gusto, and garlic cheese toast. And a cheesecake, she added. You just couldn't have a family feast without a special dessert.

She remembered the holidays when Mandy and Sam would argue over the topping. Amanda always wanted pineapple, while Sam preferred cherries, and the women, Stephanie and Michele, always opted for chocolate drizzled over raspberries. The men were usually long gone, having situated themselves in front of a football game with beer and pretzels as their last course.

She recalled the time the four of them had built the deck on Kevin and Michele's first home. Both Stephanie and Michele were in the family way and were little more than supervisors for the project. It had been Michele's self-imposed job to pull the paper tag off the ends of the pressure treated lumber. The men could have cared less whether they were left on or not, but Michele, little perfectionist that she was, couldn't stand looking at the unsightly tags, so she worked at pulling them all off until she managed to prick her finger on one of the staples. When her finger wouldn't stop bleeding, Kevin had enlisted his brother's aid for his medical expertise.

"Direct pressure. Just keep direct pressure on it."

"That's not working, Michael. What next?" Kevin had asked in an aggravated state.

"Oh, for crying out loud," Michael had replied as he leveraged himself off the end of the sawhorse he'd been kneeling on.

He'd been trying to trim a piece of wood and this was the third cut that hadn't turned out right.

He walked over to Michele, examined her bleeding finger, and took her into the house to take care of it.

They'd emerged ten minutes later with Michele bandaged well past the elbow.

She could still see the look of shock on Kevin and Stephanie's faces. The laughter all of them shared over Michael's greatly exaggerated care still rang in her ears if she listened for it.

Michele smiled to herself. Michael and Sam coming to visit unexpectedly on Saturday would be the perfect time to take Mandy aside and tell her about the baby. It would also be a good time to remind her of her family ties, to let her know that she was well-loved, not just by her mother and grandmother, but by her uncle and her cousin, both of whom were doing their part to help save her life. She needed to know that.

She quickly read through a few recipes in her cookbooks, then grabbed her purse and went out through the garage to her car. After going to the grocery store, maybe she'd stop at the wine shop. Just because she couldn't drink didn't mean Michael couldn't, and she remembered how much he loved a good Chianti with his pasta.

Saturday morning, Michele woke with a new spring in her step. Her first thought every morning was of the new life growing inside her. That always made her smile, but this morning her smile was even brighter. She couldn't really explain it, but she couldn't wait to see Michael, to see if her memory was doing him justice. To see how close the man she was beginning to conjure up every night and every morning came to the man he actually was right now. Just how long had it been since they'd actually seen each other, she wondered. Over a year, but not quite two? When had it been actually? Then she remembered. It had been the Christmas before last when Michael and Sam had come to San Francisco for a medical conference and he'd extended the trip to visit them. The sight of him had pained her for a few minutes, as his face was Kevin's almost exactly. They had always worn their hair differently, and Kevin had a jauntiness to his walk while Michael's was more sedate, but other than that they were identical to anyone who didn't really know them.

The more subtle differences were picked up only by those who were around them all the time: the sexy cleft in the middle of their chins—Kevin's had been more pronounced; the piercing gray-blue eyes they'd both inherited—Kevin's tended more toward steely blue while Michael's were a soft pewter; and their skin and hair coloring quite often set them apart. Kevin had taken the time on layovers to lay out by hotel pools and bask in the sun so his skin had a perpetual deep tan. Michael, who was outside only on ski weekends and was scrupulous about sunscreen, was tan but not bronzed. And of course, the same hours in the sun bleached and streaked Kevin's chestnut-colored hair two or three shades lighter.

Both men had turned many an eye though, singularly or in tandem. Michele couldn't help but remember with pride the day that Kevin had chosen her to be his bride. A shiver ran through her as she recalled how romantic that night had been as they dined and danced at the Mark Hopkins. For dessert there had been the light blue box with the satin lining, open and inviting under a silver-domed serving dish. It seemed to her at the time that the whole restaurant had been in on the surprise. The dashing young man in his pilot's uniform, kneeling beside the table, imploringly looking up to a lovely, coquettish woman who had tears in her eyes.

She stood at the sink, toothbrush in hand, and assessed herself. How would Michael think she had held up these past two years? She turned her head slightly and touched the tiny crinkles at the corner of her eye. Those hadn't been there, she was sure. Neither had those touches of light gray at her hairline, the ones that her stylist had so cleverly camouflaged with highlights. Her eyes were still clear and lovely, that she had to admit. They were bright, intense, and dark-lashed under nicely sculpted brows.

She had read once that a famous researcher of sexual physiology, one who had written seven books on the subject, had deemed that a woman's eyes were her number one asset in the chase game, her hair, number two. If that was truly the case, she had the first two bases completely covered. Her eyes were capable of stopping men in their tracks, her hair, when taken care of, was silky and thick enough to invite a lingering touch. Her lips were full and bow-shaped, showing off carefully cared-for teeth. Her father, a dentist, had insisted on her brushing after every meal, and she still did so to this day. Her cheekbones were prominent but not overly so, needing only a slight dusting of blush to set them off. And her pert little nose with the freckles on the tip went well with everything else that was framed by her small heart-shaped face. She had a classic beauty that had softened like a flower opening.

No, not too shabby. But the body was going downhill daily. You really couldn't tell any difference when she was dressed, but naked, in front of a mirror, she noticed hips splaying out slightly, and a waist that was thickening. Her breasts, always ample, were now straining against the fabric of her dresses and sweaters. If this early stage was any indication of how her pregnancy was going to progress in terms of size, she would be gargantuan before this was all over.

Thank God she didn't have to worry about morning sickness. She hadn't with Amanda either, but she had dearly paid for the cushy first and second trimesters with an absolutely brutal labor and delivery. Patting her slightly-rounded tummy, she sighed. The weight was something she could deal with later. Much later, after she was assured that Mandy was fully recovered.

She finished brushing her teeth and took a long shower. As her hands roamed over her body, noticing the slight changes, she tried to let her mind slip into what she thought a man's frame of mind might be. Full, curvy, and plump. Definitely plump there on the hip. She ran her hand over her back side and hip again. Oh yes, she definitely had hips now. Then her soapy hands massaged her breasts. She felt over the mounds of flesh for lumps as she often did. Yes, they were larger. And tender, too. She fondly remembered Kevin's fascination with her "jugs of distinction." Oh, how she missed having a man's arms around her. A man touching her and a man to share things with. A man whose physical force could plunge deep enough into her to drive out the demons of the lonely, terrifying nights that women in grief grow accustomed to.

She chose a short skirt that would show off her legs. She was petite, so they weren't as long as most men liked, but they were shapely and in proportion to her size. She topped that with a ribbed sweater that stretched to accommodate instead of making her breasts feel bound to her chest. Then she leaned over and used a bristled brush to fluff up her hair from underneath as her hairdresser had shown her. She sprayed her special jasmine fragrance up into the air and walked under it to settle the mist delicately over her. Popping two prenatal vitamins in her mouth and washing them down with her cold decaffeinated coffee, she grinned back at herself. *You've got the bloom*, she told herself, that special, hormonal, chemical thing that is a woman boasting she's satisfied with the state of her burgeoning body.

She was ready to face the day. After fixing a big breakfast for Mandy and Gabby, who was spending the weekend, she would get busy on making her special spaghetti sauce. Then, she'd make the cheesecake and get the vegetables ready for the antipasto. She would make the dressing with Michael when he got here in the late afternoon. They'd have to start establishing some new traditions. Kevin would want them to make it together, and Stephanie . . . well, Stephanie would want her to have an extra helping of the cheesecake covered with raspberries and drizzled with a rich, dark chocolate sauce.

Breakfast was a French toast casserole stuffed with cinnamon and pecans and coated with confectioner's sugar then drenched with butter and maple syrup. The girls just loved the gooey confection and Michele loved the way it made her kitchen smell homey and inviting. Why was every thought this morning somehow related to Michael and his arrival later today?

The girls seemed a little unsettled and asked a few questions about her plans for later in the day. Did they suspect anything, she wondered? But she sloughed it off; the only way they could know is if they'd overheard her phone conversation yesterday when they'd been in school.

"I'm planning to make a big dinner. I'm in the mood to cook, so I'm going to stay in the kitchen all day. I'm even going to make a cheesecake, from scratch. Why are you asking?"

"No reason," Mandy mumbled, "just curious what you were going to be up to. You know Gabby and I. Hey, we don't want to eat early tonight. We're going to walk over to the new Chrysler dealership this afternoon and check out all the cars that are for sale. Maybe once you're finally convinced that I'm over the dizzy spells, you'll let me get a car."

"Mandy, we've talked about this over and over again. Once you go six months without an episode, then you still have three months of driver's ed, then another six months of supervised driving, then you'll get a car. But no harm in looking I guess. Just don't sic any salesmen on me, all right? I'm looking forward to a nice relaxing day in the kitchen."

"Okay. So dinner won't be any earlier than say, seven, right?"

"Sure, that's fine with me. Seven it is." *Michael and Sam should certainly be here by then*, she thought. "And Gabby, your mom called this morning. She said they'd be home tomorrow night around six and that I was to make sure you fed the cat this morning."

"Yes, Mrs. M. I will. In fact, we'll go do it now. There are a few videos that Mandy and I want to get that are over there anyway."

"Okay. Make sure you lock up before you come back."

"Will do."

While Michele plopped ripe tomatoes into a big pot of boiling water, the girls went next door to plot their next step.

"He'll get here at six sharp, so we have to tell her by 5:30 so she can get ready," Mandy said.

"You saw her. She looked great. I vote we wait 'til the last minute or it's just going to be that much sooner that she freaks out at us over all this."

"You don't know that. She might really be happy about this."

"I'm not seeing it that way. I think she's going to split a gut."

"Okay, 5:45. That'll give her time to brush her teeth and comb her hair while she yells at us."

"Deal. And you tell her."

"Me?"

"Yeah. She won't yell as much if she thinks this was all your doing."

"Oh great," Gabby said with a sigh. "Just great."

At three o'clock the girls took a bus downtown to check out the new dealership. At 4:15, Michael and Sam pulled up to the curb in their rental car.

Michael could smell the zesty Italian sauce even before he reached the steps leading up to the porch. "Mmmm. Smells like old times," he said to Sam.

"Michael! Sam! Come in! Come in! Oh, it is so good to see you." One by one, Michele hugged them both tightly to her, breathing in their different scents. Sam's was an overdone Polo Sport or something trendy like that. Michael's was the familiar tangy citrus and woodsy fragrance he'd always worn that somehow smelled expensive and natural all at the same time.

Michael held her close, encompassing her warmth and unconsciously letting his hands rove familiarly over her back and hips. God, she smelled wonderful. Flowery and spicy and delicious. He kissed her neck and his lips begged to linger.

"Shelley . . . Mmmm, you smell nice."

She pulled away from his embrace and smiled up at them both. "I smell like your favorite dinner. You men and your appetites!"

As he stood there drinking in the sight of her, he suddenly realized that he did have an appetite, but it wasn't for food.

He handed her a wrapped box with a large bow and whispered, "Don't open it until later and then I'll tell you what they're for."

She gave him a quizzical look with one dark eyebrow raised. "Okay, I'll put it away for later," she said as she took it from him and turned to go back into the house.

Michael watched her hips swish back and forth as he followed her down the long hallway and into the kitchen. His appetite was whetted all right, he thought to himself. Had she always looked this good? And if so, how had he missed it? The self-imposed blinders of a faithful and contented husband, he supposed and smiled. When Stephanie had been alive, he'd had no reason to admire another woman's beauty. But now, interestingly enough, his eye was being drawn to this woman, this woman who was carrying his child, or more likely, children. That reminded him of one of the reasons he had flown in this afternoon. He would be taking her to the hospital tomorrow for her first sonogram. He'd already arranged it, but he hadn't told her.

"Sam, do you remember where everything is? Help yourself to a soda. The TV in the den is already hooked up to video games. If you'd like to use the computer, it's on sleep mode in my office. I remember how you used to like Tetris. I downloaded a real challenging version for you last night." She tossed the package on the window seat after giving it a surreptitious shake. Michael chuckled at her curiosity.

"Thanks. I think I'll just chill with the TV for right now. Do you have any juice?"

"Yeah. Top shelf."

She watched as Sam opened the door to the fridge and helped himself to a tall glass of orange juice. She looked at Michael and mouthed the word, "Juice?"

Michael just shrugged. Eating and drinking healthy had become a new thing with Sam lately. He hadn't wanted to draw attention to it by asking questions.

Sam asked for permission to take his drink into the family room and Michele nodded. When he was out of earshot, she commented, "Geez, I've never known him to opt for juice over a can of soda. What did you do with the real Sam?"

Michael laughed. "You got me. One week, I was at the store buying Sun Drop by the case and the next, I was buying any juice that wasn't reconstituted. I think this medical stuff is seeping in. I only hope his dentist doesn't start picketing."

Michele laughed and patted his hand. A warm tingle traveled up her arm and she instantly stopped laughing. They both looked over at each other and their eyes locked. In the moments of silence they could hear the small popping sounds coming from the sauce bubbling in the large pot on the stove.

Then Michael opened his arms and reached for her and she fell into them. They embraced and held each other tightly, neither wanting to let go. And neither understanding just exactly why that was.

They stepped away from each other when they heard Sam coming back into the room. "Hey, where's Manda? Oh, sorry . . . ." He turned to go away.

"Wait. Sam. Don't go. We're just being sentimental." Using her apron, she wiped at a tear in her eye. "Mandy's with Gabby. They went into town to this new Chrysler dealership that just opened. They both have pipe dreams about getting a car."

"Oh."

"They should be back soon. They wanted me to plan dinner for seven o'clock, but I told them to be back by six. I didn't tell them you were coming, I wanted to surprise them. Do you remember Gabby, Sam?"

"No, I don't think so. I think I'd remember a name like Gabby. Does she talk too much?"

"No," Michele laughed. "It's short for Gabriella, just as Mandy is short for Amanda."

"Manda's what I always called her."

"Yeah, I know. She's going to be thrilled to see you! I can't wait."

Michele turned back to the stove and stirred the sauce. Then she passed the wooden spoon over to Michael for him to taste.

"Ummm," he said as his eyes closed. "Just like I remember."

"Well, you'd better roll those sleeves up and wash those hands, 'cause I'm counting on you to make the antipasto and the dressing just like *I* remember."

"Don't have my partner," Michael said sadly. "The one who ate more olives than he stuffed," he said with a smile.

"I know. And I'm a poor substitute. But I promise not to eat the olives before the salad is served."

"Good deal," he said as he removed his blazer and started rolling up his sleeves. "Sam, you want to help?"

"No thanks, Dad. I think I will try out that Tetris game until Manda gets here."

"Okay, we'll call you."

When they were alone in the kitchen again, Michael asked her how she was feeling. He was washing his hands and Michele smiled as she noted how thorough he was. He was a surgeon, even unconsciously.

"Actually Michael, I feel pretty darned wonderful. Haven't had a moment of nausea, no anxiety, and I'm sleeping like normal again. Eight hours most nights. I can hardly believe it."

"Well, you look marvelous. You haven't changed a bit. Still lovely as ever."

"Thank you, Michael. And thank you for the baby, too."

Michael had turned and braced his hands behind him on the counter after washing up, now he impatiently pushed away from it and threw the towel down on the counter. "Damn it! I can't wait!"

"What?"

He grabbed his blazer from the doorknob where he'd just left it and took her by the hand. Then he pulled her with him toward the door, calling up the stairs as he went. "Sam, we're going to the hospital for a few minutes. Wait for the girls. We won't be long."

"Hospital?" Sam called down. "Something wrong?"

"No, don't worry. Watch the sauce on the stove, it's simmering on low."

"Hospital?" she asked.

"Yes, I arranged a sonogram for tomorrow, but I don't want to wait any longer. So we're going now."

"Now?" she asked as he pulled her through the door. She managed to untie her apron and throw it onto one of the rocking chairs on the porch as he dragged her along with him.

"Now. I want to know. I just want to know."

"Want to know what?"

"Everything. How many. If they're all right. If you're all right."

"Michael, I'm fine. Really."

He opened the car door for her, waited until she was settled inside, and then quickly went around to the driver's side.

"I need to be reassured. It's hard worrying long distance."

Ten minutes later they were at the hospital, and twenty minutes later they were in a private room with a technician, who was awed to have such a noted and respected physician helping him set up and run the fairly routine test.

Michele was a little unnerved and embarrassed when Michael unceremoniously pulled both the waistband of her panties and the elastic around her skirt down past her hips. Both men were now looking down at her exposed abdomen. Then the technician squirted a cold, clear jelly over most of the exposed area and Michael started palpating and strumming from one side to the other. All the while, she could see one lone, dark pubic hair poking over the stark white border of her panties. She wanted to reach down and tuck it under, but she resisted calling attention to it, in the unlikely event that neither had even noticed.

The gel they were using was cold and slimy, but soon she wasn't giving it any thought as all her attention went to the lighted screen beside her. Michael held her hand and together they watched as the technician moved the transducer in his hand. Twice Michael told him to stop and Michele strained to see what Michael was seeing, but she couldn't make out anything. Finally, she heard him let out a huge sigh, and then he instructed the technician to start over while he talked.

"Shelley, let me show you your babies."

"Babies?"

"Babies, honey. Ready?"

"Yes," she said, smiling up at him and squeezing his hand.

As the technician moved his hand, Michael used his other one to point out each baby on the screen. "This one is turned sideways, see?"

She nodded, even though she really didn't see a baby, just a grayish shadow.

"And here's another . . . ." His finger outlined a blob that was moving slightly. "And another . . . ."

"Another!"

"And another . . . ."

Michael felt Michele's hand fall from his and he spun to look down at her. "Shit! She's passed out. Get me an ammonia wick!"

The technician gave him a small, gauze-covered glass vial and Michael expertly broke it with his thumb and waved it under Michele's nose.

"Unhh. Unhhn," she moaned, as she turned her head away from the noxious odor.

"Honey. Wake up. Shh. Shh. Everything's okay."

"Michael . . ." she said as she smiled up into his face—until she remembered why it was that she had passed out in the first place.

"Michael, four?"

He smiled down at her and leaned over to kiss her cheek. "Yes. Four."

Her hand went to her head and rested there while the technician, with Michael's help, cleaned the gel from her abdomen. Then the technician, sensing that he was unwanted and unneeded, left the room. Just before reaching the door, he came back, flipped a switch on a control panel, and offered something to Michael. Michael glanced down, smiled, and pocketed the picture that the technician had just handed him. He thanked him for fitting them in with no notice and then turned to help Michele with her clothes. After she was finished adjusting her skirt and panties, he lifted her off the table. His large hands held her securely and he kept her close to his side to make sure she was over the effects of her fainting spell.

"Gee, you don't feel heavy enough to be carrying four," he joked.

She gave him a sideways smile and then the tears started to come.

"Hey, what's this?" he asked as he caught one on its way down her cheek.

"Michael, four babies! What am I going to do with four babies!"

"Love them. Feed them, clothe them, educate them. Same as you'd do for one."

"Suddenly I'm overwhelmed."

"Suddenly, I'm sorry I didn't get a waiver for my attorney."

Her face jerked up until her eyes met his, and when she saw the big smile on his face, she grinned too.

"What a pickle," she muttered as he helped her find her shoes.

"Well, look at it this way, we're bound to have the match Mandy needs."

"Yeah," and her eyes brightened and her smile widened. "Yeah." This was, after all, about Mandy first, and now Mandy was practically assured to be home free.

"Come on, let me take you home and you can tell her that her mother's become a brood mare."

"Hey, that's not funny."

"Yeah, it is," he said with a chuckle. "Yeah, it most definitely is."

On the way back home, they both let their thoughts have free rein as they adjusted to the idea of quadruplets. By the time they actually got back to the house they were both almost punch drunk with laughter from the quips they had been tossing back and forth.

"And you'll be able to get group discounts for the movies and bowling."

"You know, you've really been a big help today. The only thing I asked you to do was help make the salad, but did you do that? No, you didn't even do that. Instead you helped out by letting me know, that soon, I'll have to set the table for four more!"

As he helped her out of the car, he smiled down at her. "Now, aren't you glad that I came to help you tell Mandy? I grabbed a few more of those ammonia capsules, just in case we need them."

She playfully slapped him on the shoulder. The hard feel of his muscle and the instantaneous heat she felt from touching him shocked her. "Looks like the girls are back."

Sam and Gabby were sitting in rocking chairs side by side and Mandy sat on the top porch step. When she saw them coming up the walk, she stood up and gave her uncle a big hug. "Uncle Michael, this is a nice surprise!"

"You haven't seen anything yet, sweetheart," he said as he lifted her completely off the ground and swung her around. As he spun her, he saw Michele give him an admonishing look. It apparently wasn't time to tell anybody yet.

"Mom, I have to talk to you in private," she looked down at her watch. Five minutes of six. "Like right away, please."

"Sure, honey. What's the matter?"

"Uhh . . . you're not going to believe this," she said as she followed her mom into the house, "but, uhhh . . . you've got a date in like five minutes."

"What?"

While Mandy was in the kitchen telling her mother what she'd been up to, Gabby was on the porch filling Sam and Michael in on Michele's soon-to-be arrival. They could hear Michele's loud outburst as it funneled down the long corridor and out onto the porch.

"Amanda! I can't believe you did this!"

"Well, I did. And he's going to be here any minute now."

Mandy and her mother stood, hands on their hips, staring each other down mutinously.

They heard Gabby and Sam say that they were going for a walk, and then they heard Michael come into the house and go upstairs. Moments later they heard someone's heavy tread on the front steps. It sounded like booted feet reverberating on the porch decking, and then they heard the doorbell ring.

"He's here, Mom! He's here. You've got to get the door!"

"Well, I'll answer the door, but I'm not going out on a date with a perfect stranger!"

"Please Mom. You have to."

"No, I don't!"

"Well, you at least have to go to the door and meet him," she said wistfully.

Michele gave Mandy a hard stare that had fury on top of fury burning in it. "Fine, I'll go meet him, but then I'm telling him to go home," she hissed.

She walked down the hallway to the front door trying very hard not to stomp or swing her fists in anger.

She opened the screen door and invited the man in.

"Hi, I'm Michele Moore. You must be . . . ."

"Milo. Milo Markovitch, remember?" A look of pure pleasure crossed his face as he looked her up and down, and she wondered just for a moment what he had been expecting.

"Oh yes. Yes, now I remember." She turned and looked daggers at Mandy. "How could I possibly forget? Milo, please come in. I'm afraid I'm not quite ready yet. Can you give me a minute or two?"

"Sure, sure. Take all the time you need. Nice place you've got here."

"Thank you. Thank you very much. Mandy? Mandy, why don't you come and keep Mr. Markovitch company while I go upstairs for a minute?"

"Milo, my daughter Amanda."

"Yeah, I remember your profile said you had a daughter. Hi Amanda. So you doin' good in school?"

"Uh. Yeah. I'm doing fine in school."

"I'll be down in a few minutes," Michele said as she ran up the stairs. In the hallway, she collided with Michael.

"Michael. What am I going to do? Amanda's gone and . . . ."

"I know what Amanda's been up to. Gabby filled us in."

"What am I going to do? I can't go out with him!"

"Why not? He looks nice." He had a huge grin on his face and she couldn't help believing that he was enjoying this immensely.

"Michael!" she said and pushed hard against his chest. "Don't be ridiculous! This is the last thing I need today! I'm hardly over the shock I got an hour ago and now this?"

"Okay, okay. I'll take care of it. Call Amanda up here and I'll go down and talk to him."

"Oh thank you, Michael."

He kissed her lightly on the temple and said, "Call Amanda."

"Amanda, sweetheart," she called with sickening sweetness, "could you come up here for a moment please?"

As Amanda slowly trudged up the stairs, painstakingly gripping the banister, Michael stepped to the opposite side and went down. He smiled and winked at her as they passed each other, but she was too agitated to acknowledge it.

"Mr. Markovitch. I'm Dr. Moore, Michele's brother-in-law. We need to talk, can I get you a drink?"

"Yeah, sure. Bud, if you got it. Otherwise it don't matter. I don't like the light stuff though."

"Come with me into the kitchen and let's see what Michele has."

Ten minutes later, they all watched as Milo got in his big black pickup truck and pulled abruptly away from the curb. Michele and Mandy watched from an upstairs window and Michael, from the front screen door.

Michele slowly came down the stairs. "What did you say to him?"

"Well, I just chitchatted for a while, telling him I was real happy you were seeing somebody else other than me."

"And what did he say to that?"

"He asked me why, so I told him the truth. That seeing's how I got you knocked up and seeing's how you were carrying four of my babies, I sure could use a little help from another income to reduce the child support payments I'd be making."

Michele gaped openmouthed at him for a moment, stunned at Michael's words. Then her eyes met his twinkling, dark gray ones and they both laughed hard and hardy. Finally, catching her breath, she croaked, "Just get in the kitchen and make my salad dressing. I swear, this day is definitely going to be on the front pages in the baby memories book!"

Mandy, apparently afraid to leave her room, heard them laughing, but not quite ready to face the music, she let Michael and Michele finish fixing dinner alone.

It was a nice time of catching up and coloring in the emotions they had suffered and shared over the years. Michele couldn't remember the last time she had laughed so much and Michael couldn't remember the last time a woman's laughter had affected him so oddly.

Though it was delegated off to a corner of their minds, they were both constantly aware of the big news of the day.

Their individual thoughts returned to it privately and repeatedly as they each tried to adjust and settle their feelings.

When dinner was ready, they feasted on a salad of crisp radicchio, arugula, and romaine leaves topped with strips of Genoa salami, thin slices of prosciutto, and spicy circles of pepperoni. Whole chunks of buffalo mozzarella, provolone, and Gorgonzola cheeses lined the oversized platter along with black and Kalamata olives stuffed with pimento and dill. There was an assortment of marinated portabella mushrooms, roasted red peppers, Roma tomatoes, and pickled onions, all drizzled with Michael and Kevin's fresh-crushed basil, garlic, and Parmesan dressing. Then Michele served her special spaghetti sauce with the traditional blend of capellini and fettuccini pastas.

The first time she had made the dish for the whole, extended family many years ago, she hadn't had enough of either kind of pasta and had mixed the two kinds together. Now, that was the only way it could be served. Traditions being what they are—mistakes that turned out well, or disasters memorable for whatever reasons—continued to be repeated for everyone's heckling or genuine pleasure.

After dinner, by prior arrangement, Sam offered to take Gabby to the mall to see a movie. When Mandy, confused by Sam's attempt to single her out, said she wanted to go too, Michele put her arm around her daughter's shoulders and walked her into the family room where Michael was watching the news.

"I'm being punished aren't I? That's why I can't go with them, isn't it?" Mandy said sullenly.

As soon as Michael saw Michele sit Mandy down in a chair, he reached for the remote and turned off the television. Mandy was looking dejectedly at her twisting fingers, her eyes lowered to the carpet. She was fearing and dreading the punishment that she knew was coming.

"I was only trying to get you out on a date!"

"This isn't about that. I know you had good intentions, even though what you did was a very, very bad idea."

"I thought she showed resourcefulness," Michael commented as he winked over at Mandy. Michele shot him a quelling look and he looked down at the carpet, too.

"Amanda, Uncle Mike and I have something we need to talk to you about and it's better if Gabby and Sam aren't here."

Amanda looked anxiously back and forth between the adult faces.

"What? What's the matter now? It's another doctor isn't it?" she said with undisguised disgust and contempt.

"Well, yeah, it is for a while, at least for your mother," Michael said slowly.

At the news that her mother needed a doctor, Mandy's head jerked up and her panicked eyes searched her out. "Mom? What's wrong, Mom? What is it?" she practically screamed.

Michele took Amanda's hand and moved to sit beside her on the couch. Then she lightly patted it between hers. "There's nothing wrong with me, per se. In fact, all things considered, everything is right as rain right now."

She took a deep breath and blurted out, "I'm pregnant, Mandy. In fact, I'm very pregnant. I'm going to have quadruplets about five or six months from now."

"You're pregnant? But, how . . . . Quad? Isn't that four? I don't understand." She was shaking her head like she was trying to clear a fog.

Michael leaned forward and put his hands together in front of his spread knees. "A few months ago, your mother read about a procedure that could benefit you greatly. It could even save your life. That's what we're counting on anyway. Rich blood cells from umbilical cords are being used every day to save the lives of people with diseases like yours. Well, naturally, knowing your mother, she had to try everything in her power to make you better, and then in her typical fashion, she had to do it one better, or in this case, three better. And yes, quad means four. She's got four babies growing in here," he said as he leaned over and patted her familiarly on the belly.

"Four? Four? And how? Who?"

"Well, that's where I came into play. The best chances for this procedure require tissue typing as close to the recipient's as possible. Your dad being my twin made me the most likely candidate. And it was my idea to boost your mother's egg production to better her chances of carrying a baby as close as possible to your typing. We may have gone a little overboard with four," he said with chagrin.

"We? You and she?" she asked in alarm.

Michele jumped in then and said, "No, no, he and I, we didn't . . . ."

"The babies were conceived by artificial insemination. I sent sperm from Denver to her doctor here."

Mandy stood and slowly paced the room. "This is so odd. You guys are making all this up, right?"

"No, honey," Michele said simply. "No. We're not making it up. I am pregnant and we just found out a few hours ago that there are four babies. So, we're all adjusting to the shock right now."

"Shock is right! I appreciate you doing all this for me, but what are we going to do with four babies?"

Michele and Michael turned and just looked at each other. There was silence in the room for several moments as they both realized the impact this was going to have on all of them. Then Michele slowly stood up and walked over to where Mandy stood by the fireplace. "We're going to love them and take care of them. You always wanted a brother or a sister."

"One! Not four! And not all at one time! And that was years ago. Now we won't even be in the same generation! Four! Four!"

"Yeah, well we didn't have a lot of choice in that matter. With one, Michael didn't feel we'd have the odds in our favor. This way, we can practically be sure one of the babies will match up to you. Mandy, this could cure you. From everything I've read, this is the most successful thing going on in the field of medicine right now. The success rate is phenomenal. Honey, you're going to get better, I just know it."

The words were taking time to sink in, but finally, Mandy was realizing all the implications. "What if I don't make it six months," she tossed out. "Then you've had four babies for nothing!"

Michele took her daughter in her arms and hugged her. "You're going to make it baby, I know you are. Women with multiples usually deliver early and we're going to take the absolute best care of you. You'll be in the hospital the same time as I am, and as soon as the babies are delivered, the cord that's most promising will be rushed off to a team of doctors who will get everything ready for you. By the time I come home from the hospital, so will you. Completely cured if all goes well. And I'm sure that everything will. I feel it."

"Mom, you're going to get as big as a house!"

"Gee, thanks."

"You know what I mean. You're going to be huge. How will you even get around? Who's going to take care of four babies? This isn't going to work."

"Mandy, I'm sure it's going to take a little while for you to get used to this. I'm not even used to the idea of all this myself yet. But we're going to do just fine. I'll probably have to hire someone to help us when the time comes, but that's okay, we'll manage. And it'll be fun. Babies are lots of fun."

"Oh yeah, right. Mom, you just keep thinking that. I think you're delusional. Remember last year when Gabby and I each had a twenty-four hour prototype baby for a week? You just about went through the roof every time it cried. Imagine that times four. And for weeks without end. Mom, I hate to say this, but I think this was a big mistake. A very, very big mistake."

"Be that as it may," Michele said, a new firmness in her voice, "that's the way it is. I wasn't about to let this opportunity pass without giving it a shot. You mean the world to me and if it meant I'd have to have fifty babies, I'd still do it! So I expect you to be more supportive after the shock wears off. Now why don't you go to your room so you can start getting a handle on all this, because I *am* pregnant, and there's nothing I can do about it now. You'll just have to accept the fact that we have babies on their way and *one* of them is going to change the course of your life, if we're lucky!"

"Fine! I'll go to my room. But don't think I'm happy about this! Even though you did this for me, I think it was a stupid thing to do!" she said as she stomped up the stairs.

"So was hawking me on the Internet!" Michele yelled up the landing after her.

"I was just trying to leave you with somebody to love after I was gone!" she hollered back just before they heard the door slam.

"Well, I think that went real well, how about you?" Michael said.

"Just dandy," she replied as she plopped down beside him and let her head fall back against the top cushion of the sofa.

"Here," he said as he picked up her feet and swung them around. "Might as well get used to putting your feet up." He tossed her a pillow to put under her head and placed her feet in his lap. Then he removed her shoes and began massaging her feet.

"Oh, that feels wonderful Michael. You have the hands of a god."

"That's what all my patients say, but somehow, it sounds better coming from you."

She closed her eyes and enjoyed the feeling of relaxing completely as Michael continued to rub her feet, her ankles, and her calves.

"She'll come around."

"I know. This was way out of the blue for her. She'll probably be bouncing off the walls tomorrow, anxious to go to school on Monday to tell all her friends."

"Well, I'm not sure I'd count on all that. Speaking of friends, Sam and Gabby seem to be hitting it off for the moment. When I originally asked him to take Gabby aside, he acted like it would be a real hardship. I actually had to pay him. But since he met her this afternoon, it doesn't seem that he's had any problems keeping her all to himself."

"Gabby's nice people. She's been wonderful these past two years. She even cut her hair atrociously short when Mandy was losing hers. She wanted to shave it, but I wouldn't let her go that far. I think her mother was relieved. But she does look rather cute with it short and spiky."

"It's good that Amanda has a friend like that. How about you? Do you have a friend like that?"

"I did. Once upon a time. His name was Kevin."

"Yeah, he was my friend, too. I miss him."

"Do you think he'd be proud of us?"

"Most definitely. Four babies? Hell, I'm proud of me!"

She laughed a delightful little laugh and he felt something inside him curl and open. Looking down he smiled at the happy little mother. Well, she wouldn't be little for much longer. He reached up with his hand and rubbed her lower abdomen.

She looked up and stared into his deep blue-gray eyes. Was the reason she was letting him be so familiar because he was a doctor, or because he was the father of the babies she carried? Or was it because of something else? Some other reason of propriety that she had yet to name?

His hands continued to lightly caress her and within minutes, she was sound asleep.

"That was some scary movie!" Gabby exclaimed as she and Sam walked the length of the long suburban block. He had to park the rental car almost at the end of it because of the shortage of on-street parking.

"Yeah, my fingers are still numb from where they were pinched together when you were gripping them so tightly!"

"Sorry, I have to do something. Usually I bite my nails."

He picked up her hand and looked at her fingernails. "Either it's been a while since you went to a movie or the last movie was a comedy."

"It was a romance. Nothing as tense as tonight's."

"Generally, I find the notion of romance even more horrifying than vampires, werewolves, or specters."

"Why's that?"

"Girls don't go for me. They think I'm too nerdy. The school that I go to, anyone with a brain is considered geeky and undateable, while those who smoke, drink, drive too fast, and do drugs are *de rigueur*. It's a weird school. I don't have many friends. I'm known as the 'doc's dork.' And of course, it doesn't help that I'm six foot four."

"Wow, here you'd be a real catch."

"Really?"

"Really. Look at you, you're a sharp dresser. Everything you're wearing screams affluent, well-to-do . . . preppy almost. Just looking at you a girl can see your confidence. You have that I'm-going-to-the-right-college and I'm-going-to-make-something-of-myself attitude that makes the money girls sit up and take notice."

"You really think so?"

"Yeah. I think so. So they'd better watch out. I saw you first," she said with a bright smile.

Still holding her hand in his, he bent over it and kissed each finger.

She felt each shiver go up her arm, down her spine, and end up somewhere behind her knee where it threatened to collapse her.

"I had a good time tonight," he whispered.

"Me, too."

"I'm having a little problem here, though."

"Yeah, what's that?"

"Since you're staying in the same house as I am tonight, I'm trying to figure out where I'm supposed to kiss you good night."

She looked up at him, way up at him, as there was easily more than a foot difference in their heights. "May I suggest the porch steps since I believe we're going to need to be on different levels?"

He laughed heartily and led her up the pathway to the porch steps. Then he easily lifted her to the one above him and cupped her face with his hands. His eyes looked deeply into hers and then they moved lower to where her lips were. He closed his eyes and ever so gently placed his lips over hers. If she hadn't already guessed that this was his first real kiss, she would have thought he was terribly lacking in finesse. But having decided that it probably was his first real kiss as well as their very first kiss together, she wasn't ready to accept it being mediocre. She reached up and wrapped her arms around his neck and pulled him down to her, forcing his lips apart with hers. She used the tip of her tongue to deftly trace the inside of his lips. When she felt him shudder and then heard him moan, she curved her lips against his and went back for more. His hands left her cheeks and wrapped around her and then as he kissed her as deeply as she was kissing him, his hands tentatively moved lower on her back. Leaning into him, she brushed her small breasts up against his chest. Instantly, his body responded and hardened against her softness.

Knowing full well what she was doing to him, she pulled away and smiled up at him. "Well, time for bed. Mandy will be wondering what I've been up to. What are you fixing for breakfast, handsome?" she asked as she walked under his arm and into the house.

He bit his tongue to keep from stuttering, because that's exactly what his mind said he was going to do if he spoke right now. "Mmmm, pancakes," he managed to get out. "I'm good at pancakes."

"Great, I'm good at eating them. 'Night," she whispered before she turned and ran up the remaining stairs.

Sam was on his way to the kitchen to get something to ease his suddenly very dry throat when he spotted his father sitting on the sofa. Closer examination revealed a sleeping Aunt Shelley half on, half off his lap, so he detoured and sat across from him in an overstuffed armchair.

"So, how'd it go?" he whispered over to his father.

"Great. Mandy's just thrilled with the idea," he said with enough sarcasm that his son could easily pick up on it.

"Hmmm. Well, this is probably going to take some time for her to get used to. It would me."

"We did the sonogram today. There's four."

"No shit! Sorry. No kidding?"

"No shit. No kidding. No April Fool's. Four."

"Wow."

"Yeah. Wow." He looked down at the sleeping woman in his lap. "I've been downplaying it all day for her sake, but this scenario probably isn't all that good. She's a very tiny woman, who had one hell of a difficult pregnancy the last time. I don't see how she can carry four babies to term."

"Hmmm. Well, as you're always saying, let nature sort things out."

"Yeah, I say that. But I don't mean it when it's my things that are getting sorted."

"Yeah, I know."

"How was the movie?"

"Great. Gabby is terrific!"

"Glad to hear it," he said with a touch of caution. "Remember, we're leaving tomorrow afternoon."

"Yeah, I know. There's just enough time for a real quick fling," he said with bravado.

Michael smiled at his son's hubris. How a boy got to be seventeen with so little experience with girls was beyond him, but it was nice to see him finally attracted to one. And one attracted to him.

"It's getting late, but I'm not tired enough to sleep yet. I think I'll just sit here in the dark for a while, sorting things out in my mind." He looked down and smiled at the woman sighing and turning in his lap.

"Goodnight Dad, see you in the morning."

"Goodnight son, and thanks for your help today."

"Believe me, it was my pleasure. Oh, by the way . . . Dad?"

"Yes?"

"How do you make pancakes?"

When Sam finally left to go to his room, Michael looked down at the sleeping form still curled up at his hip.

She was lovely. And very, very, sweet. She had shopped and cooked her heart out for him and Sam, trying to make them feel welcome and special. He knew that she hadn't had company for a long time, so it had probably been fun for her to entertain like this, but still, she *had* gone all out. He caressed her shoulder and lightly ran his fingertips down past her waist. The movement made her arch and turn into him, and all he could see in the dim light was the outline of her full breasts pressed against the pliant sweater. God, when was the last time he'd held a woman's breast in his hand? Then he smiled at himself because the answer that came to mind was so ludicrous.

Why, it had been Mrs. McKeely's when he'd been checking her for a fevered lump. It was not unusual for a nursing mother to get a painful infection in a milk duct and to ask him about it when the baby was having its checkup. But feeling a woman clinically was worlds apart from feeling a woman sexually. And right now, he very much wanted to move his hand down Shelley's shoulder to where her breast swelled over the visible line of her bra just under the sweater. He could see the shape of her breasts in the dim light, even under the thick knit of her sweater. His fingers itched to touch her there, to define her and to heft her. He knew touching her breasts would be unlike any sensation he'd ever had.

Stephanie had been relatively small breasted. Her nipples had been quite responsive though, and he had loved holding her tight to him while he slept, one hand cupping a firm breast. He could feel himself harden, and mercilessly, Shelley took just that instant to turn into him, nudging his now fully-engorged shaft with her elbow.

"Ahhh," he muttered and purposefully rose to a standing position, taking her up in his arms with him.

"Mmmm," she sighed as her eyes slowly opened. "Where we going?" she muttered.

"Bed. We're going to bed. You to yours, me to mine." *Unfortunately*, he added in his mind, as he proceeded to carry her upstairs to her room.

As she clung softly to his shoulders, he savored the feel of her in his arms. This wasn't hateful. He could get pretty used to this he thought, as he heard the grandfather clock in the foyer bong midnight. He matched each step on the stairs with a chime and then at the top, he turned to take her to her room. Laying her gently on her bed, he removed the tiny headband from her head. She woke up and smiled up at him as he lifted her enough to pull the covers down around her. He kissed her on the cheek and then, because he wanted to know how she tasted, he kissed her on the lips. When her arms went around his neck and she murmured, "Kevin, come to bed," he firmly untangled her and stood up. Just before turning out the bedside lamp and closing her door, he saw the picture on the opposite night table.

"Kevin," he whispered, "You sure were a lucky man, for a while anyway. Now, look at us. Your wife is having my babies.

Four of them. Can you believe that? And just how the hell am I supposed to leave her here by herself with four babies?"

Sam put his arm under his head and stared at the ceiling fan in the small study that was his room for the night. He'd heard Gabby and Mandy talking in hushed whispers in the next room for the longest time, but he hadn't been able to make out a single word in all the excited gibberish coming through the paneled wall. It was quiet now and he could only assume everyone was asleep but him.

He could still feel Gabby's lips on his if he closed his eyes and concentrated. And just thinking about the way her breasts had pressed against his chest sent warm, rushing currents all through his body. So this was what love felt like! He'd never felt anything quite like it, and he was sure that if he and Gabby were the only ones in this house, he'd be trying to experience more of those tantalizing kisses, more of those wondrous touches. Clinically, he knew exactly what his body was priming for, what he was responding to, in the most elemental and hormonal way, but somehow, he sensed it was much more than that. Gabby had touched something deep inside, a chord no one had ever bothered to find.

After a particularly trying day in middle school, many years ago, he'd discovered just how shallow some girls could be when a group of them had teased him into thinking they were attracted to him, only to laugh and giggle with cruel words of rejection when he took the bait and asked one of them out. His mother had told him then, that one day, there would be a girl just for him, a girl who would be not only a best friend but a partner, and a soul mate, a girl who would make him want to play doctor, in an entirely different way.

Well, he didn't know about the partner or the soul mate part, but boy, he sure did know about the playing doctor part. His whole body was tense and hard with longing for her; his desire to explore and touch secret parts of her, not just with his hands but with his incredibly hard, throbbing maleness, was sure to keep him up most of the night.

He'd had hard-ons before, but they'd never really bothered him like this. This one would not take no as the definitive answer. Every time he tried to channel his thoughts elsewhere, he was forced back to recollections of those minutes on the porch and the burgeoning would begin again. And each succeeding time it was stronger, more fervent. He knew if he tented the covers and looked down, the silky steel of his youthful manhood would be purple in its angry single-mindedness.

He groaned out loud in his frustration and rolled over onto his stomach. Forcing his heat into the mattress, he couldn't help but stroke in tiny little circles that grew helplessly larger. *Good God*, he thought, *Aunt Shelley would certainly have a fit if he creamed himself all over her sheets.* But soon, it didn't matter; thoughts of Gabby's soft body under his took control over his erect state. Trying unsuccessfully to keep his grunts and moans low, he rode his hips into the valley he created with his hand and soon, he experienced the wonderment of his first lust-inspired release as his lips recalled Gabby's kiss.

Then, even the necessary, post-midnight trip down the chilly, dark hallway to the restroom at the opposite end of the hall couldn't dim his smile. He had a girlfriend. And whether she knew it or not, as far as he was concerned, Gabby now had a boyfriend.

"I can't believe you kissed Sam. He's like . . . well, he's like, my cousin."

"I know. And I really can't tell you what happened, but somehow we just clicked. I held his hand through most of the movie, and I gotta tell ya, I just could not wait until we got home, 'cause I just knew he was going to kiss me. I was going to *make* him kiss me."

"Yuck!"

"Yuck yourself. It was wonderful," she said dreamily. "'Course I had to help him along some. I don't think he's ever French kissed anyone."

"You're not serious!"

"I am! I'm sure he didn't know what to do when I stuck my tongue in his mouth. But believe me, he's a very fast learner!"

"I still can't believe it. You and Sam."

"Well, I can't believe what you've told me either! Your mom, pregnant! And you're going to have four brothers or sisters! How weird is that!"

"Pretty weird. Especially since they're my uncle's babies, too. I really can't get all this sorted out. This is like a nightmare."

"I think it's sweet."

"What?"

"I think your mom is terrific. Look what's she's doing for you. You should be happy, this is going to save your life."

"I'm not convinced."

"Sam says the odds are all in your favor."

"You talked with Sam about all this?" she asked, her eyes wide with shock.

"Yeah. On the way home he told me all about stem cells and that his dad paid him to take me to the movies."

"Wow, that must've made you feel like a real loser."

"No, not really. He showed me that he still had his dad's money in his pocket. He said he was going to give it back to him with interest."

"So how much is a date with the infamous Gabby worth these days?"

"His dad paid him fifty, but he said he was going to give him back a hundred."

"Speaking of money and dates, we really picked a bad day for Mom and Milo's first date, didn't we?"

"Yeah. Poor Mr. Markovitch. I can't imagine what he must be thinking of us."

"I don't think they told him anything about us. I just think they told him about the babies."

"Well that certainly is a hell of a way to put the kabosh on a first date. 'Hi, I'm Michele, I may look nice now, but in four months, I'll be as big as a cow, and in seven months, I'll be up to my eyebrows in diapers. You wanna play house with me?' Tell that to your date over dinner and I'll just bet he'll want to skip the movie."

"I don't think it was like that. I think Uncle Mike took him aside and told him . . . ."

"Told him what?"

Mandy had started laughing hysterically.

"Told him what?" Gabby asked again.

"I imagine, knowing Uncle Mike, that he told him mom was pregnant with four of *his* babies! But that he would stand down if he wanted to court her anyway! I can just hear him now. Yes, that's something he would definitely say!"

Both girls were giggling themselves silly when they heard a hoarse groan from the room beside them. They looked at each other in the semi-dark and burst out into gales of laughter. It was all too obvious, even for all their practical innocence, what had just happened in the room down the hallway.

"Look what you've done to Sam," Mandy whispered, hysterical with laughter.

"I'm proud of it," Gabby replied. "It's not every girl who can turn a guy on like that with just one kiss."

"You sure that's all you did?"

"I'm sure. Although, I gotta tell you. I was dying to have him feel me up a little."

"Gabby!"

"Shhh! That's our secret. Now, we'd better get some sleep or I'm going to look like death warmed over tomorrow and my romance with Sam will be history."

"Yeah, like you're not always gorgeous."

"Thanks, but you're the only one who thinks so."

"Well apparently Sam doesn't find you stepsister ugly."

"No, I don't think that he does," Gabby said with a smile. "'Night."

"It's *good* night."

"Not yet it's not. Although tonight was a pretty good candidate."

Michael and Sam made pancakes for breakfast the next morning, then Gabby, Mandy, and Sam were sent off to church. Lingering over coffee at the small kitchen dinette table, Michael broached the idea he'd been musing over since shaving early that morning.

"What would you think about us getting married?"

He was casually dressed in chinos with a Hilfiger pullover and Rockport loafers over bare feet. He was slouching in the chair with one leather-clad foot resting on a knee while he held part of the newspaper up from the table at an angle. If he'd said, "Let's go away to the Hamptons for the weekend," it would have seemed quite the natural thing to say.

Michele sat stunned staring at him, her coffee cup halfway to her mouth.

"Pardon? I thought you said . . . ."

"I did," he interrupted. "I said marry me."

They sat staring at each other, neither willing to let the moment and its awkwardness drop.

Finally, Michele put her coffee cup back in the saucer and smiled over at Michael.

"Michael, I can handle this. You don't need to come in and take charge."

"What if I said I want the babies to have my name?"

"They already have your name, you twit."

"Oh, yeah. I guess they do, don't they?"

"Uh huh. My last name's the same as yours. Moore."

He changed tacks. "I think the babies will do better in a family unit. You're going to need an awful lot of support when they get here. And you wouldn't have anything to worry about financially. My house is paid for, so are my cars, I'm debt free with almost five million in liquid assets. My annual salary . . . ."

"Michael," she said as she reached across the table and clasped his hand, "I don't need any money. I have more than enough to raise these kids. I haven't even touched Kevin's life insurance benefit yet. I would never have taken this on if I needed to count on you to support us."

"I want to support you. All of you. I want you and Mandy to move to Denver and live with Sam and me. That way we can be there for you. For you and Mandy, and the babies."

"Michael . . . people don't just get married because they have babies coming."

"Yeah, Michele, they do. Most of the time, they do. It happens all the time."

"Yeah, I guess you're right there. But we made these babies on *purpose*."

"People do that too, although the man doesn't always know they're making them on purpose."

"You did."

"Yes, I did. But now, I . . . ."

"You're not having regrets?" she asked with wide-eyed concern.

"No, no. Of course not. It's just . . . ."

"Listen, from the very beginning, you knew these were going to be my babies. What's changed everything?"

He threw his hands up and ran long fingers through his dark, shower-damp, curling hair.

"I don't know. I just know that I don't want to leave you like this. And I'm finding that I care. Very much, it seems."

"It doesn't surprise me that you care about the babies. Children are your weakness. They always have been."

"That's not it at all. It's *you* I care about. It's *you* I'm developing feelings for. Granted, if you weren't pregnant, I might not be rushing things like this. I'd take you out to dinner, maybe a movie, dancing, for long walks in the park, a drive-in or two where we wouldn't ever watch the movie, before proposing. But I think our relationship is defined by the babies right now and we have to catch up. Marry me, Michele. Let me be a part of everything. Share your life, and the babies' lives with me."

"Michael. I can't marry you. First of all, it wouldn't be fair. I told you from the onset that you would not have to shoulder the responsibility of my decision and I meant it. But more importantly, marriage is about love. You don't love me, I don't love you. It would be no more than two good friends setting up house together."

"And what's wrong with that?" he asked gruffly. His feelings were coming into play now and he didn't know how to handle the rejection of her words. *You don't love me, I don't love you,* kept echoing in his head like words to a Beatles' song. He looked up at Michele who was standing and gathering the dishes. She was talking over her shoulder, flatly dismissing the idea he had been so happy about earlier, as out-of-hand.

"Marrying me would be a disaster. What kind of wife would I be? Pretty soon I'll be too pregnant to be desirable and for two years after that, I'll be too tired raising five kids, plus helping you with Sam, to have much energy for anything else. You deserve much better than that Michael. If you've decided you want to remarry, you should get back out in the world and date. You could have any young, intelligent, beautiful woman that you wanted."

"But I want you," he deadpanned as if he didn't know he was implying she wasn't any of those things.

Without missing a beat, she spun around and threw a soapy dishtowel right smack in the center of his face.

As she watched the water and soap drip down his face and then onto the newspaper, she laughed. "If these babies have my aim, maybe we'll have our own softball team."

He reached up to wipe his wet brow with a napkin.

"I think you're missing a big chance to sign me on as coach. I can't imagine any team playing well without one."

"I'm just hoping that it doesn't turn out that we need a referee even more."

The subject obviously dismissed, Michele went back to the sink to do the dishes and Michael's attention returned to the newspaper. At least part of it. His eyes strayed every once in a while to check out her well-rounded bottom each time she bent to put a dish into the dishwasher.

Shortly after Mandy, Gabby, and Sam got back from church, Michael and Sam got into their rental car and left for the airport, but not before Michael gave Michele two prescriptions. "I need you to have these tests done by the end of next week. Have the results faxed to my office."

When she made to protest, he put a finger to her lips. "Not optional. And don't argue." Then he bent to kiss her lightly on the cheek and he was gone.

Later that night, Michele went on-line to check out the tests Michael had written her up for. At first, she had a hard time reading his writing. It was in the typical doctor scrawl and she had to try many different spellings before she finally had a match. Both tests were primarily concerned with placentas and determining intrauterine blood flow between babies. And both tests were invasive to a degree if they used a vaginal probe for the ultrasound.

She had promised herself upon finding out she was pregnant that no matter what, she would not terminate this life. She would take whatever baby God gave her, regardless of any defects. To her way of thinking, amniocentesis or anything like it was an unnecessary risk. Why chance an infection or any type of contamination from the outside world if there was no cause? And as far as she was concerned there *was* no cause.

When Michael called two weeks from now wondering where the tests results were, she'd tell him. Until then, she'd settle into the frame of mind of a woman who was preparing herself and her body for the most incredible of changes.

Two things took her off guard the next day. One was the call from Dr. Kay's secretary telling her that she had scheduled the tests Dr. Moore had requested and filling her in on the appointment times. And the other was rediscovering the present Michael had brought her that she had left on the breakfast nook in the kitchen.

Pulling the yellow ribbon off and tearing the paper, she opened the box. Inside were six, white, terry-cloth washcloths. *That was odd*, she thought as she unfolded each one. *Why would Michael give her washcloths?* Then she noticed the unique texture caused by the individual looped and knotted threads. High-quality, Turkish washcloths. Digging deeper, between the cloths and the tissue paper, she found a small note. "Certain parts of your body need to be made ready for this baby. Using these on your nipples twice a day starting now will make nursing a lot easier when the time comes. Pinch, pull, and polish. The cream enclosed will help with the skin stretching your tummy. Michael."

She dug around and found the small tube of ointment. She laughed out loud as she slid down onto the seat holding the stretch mark cream in one hand and a washcloth in the other. *Michael, you should have sent a gallon of this stuff! This tiny tube will be all used up in little more than a few weeks!* She sat on the upholstered bench laughing until she cried and then she wiped her eyes with the harsh terry cloth. She missed him already. God, it felt good to laugh. She'd call and cancel the appointments later, and then call him to explain why.

"You have to have those tests! I told you they weren't optional!"

"Why?"

"I'll tell you why. I only wish you'd asked before you canceled them!"

Boy, he was angry. And it scared her.

"We have to know how the babies are linked. It's crucial to know that now."

"Linked?"

"Yes, Shelley," he said, and she could have sworn there was a tone of impatience in his voice. "Pregnancies from one egg can share some placental vessels causing a problem called twin-to-twin transfusion, or TTTS. Whether or not the babies share vessels depends on the time when the eggs divide. Eggs dividing at the time of ovulation or up to three days past, are completely separate and share only genetic material. They're known as diamniotic-dichorionic or Di-Di. The amnion and chorion are the two layers of the bag of waters that fuse together. Di-Di means each baby has its own amnion and chorion—two separate sacs. Twins like that don't share any vessels and don't develop TTTS.

"Eggs that split three to eight days after ovulation create diamniotic-monochorionic twins. Each baby having its own amnion or diamnionic but sharing a single chorion or monchorionic, meaning that each baby has its own placenta but shares some vessels with the other. These twins are at risk for TTTS. Eggs that divide day eight to day thirteen, live in the same bag of water, have one placenta and share a single amnion and chorion and are called monoamnionic-monochorionic or Mo-Mo for short. These babies are at very high risk. They usually die from cord entanglement. But they have a low risk for TTTS. Less than 2 percent of twin pregnancies from a single egg are monoamnionic-monochorionic."

"What's twin-to-twin syndrome, and why didn't you tell me about all this before?"

"TTTS occurs only in diamniotic-monochoronic twins and only 15 percent of Di-Mo twins even develop this problem. So we don't need to worry about it now, we just have to test for it. And I didn't tell you all this before because I thought you'd just do as I asked and have the damned test!"

"What is it?" she persisted.

"What is what?"

"This TTTS."

"It's when one baby gives the other baby part of his or her blood volume and doesn't receive enough back in return. It can cause many complications, some mild some rather severe. Severe forms require laser surgery in the second trimester. There are many things that can happen, but there are also many ways that these things can be managed, *if we know about them,* " he emphasized.

"Like what other things? What else are you testing me for that I don't know about?"

"I just want to make sure what we're dealing with here. I want to know about the placentas. I want to be assured the placentas have implanted themselves properly and that everything is working as it should. That's why I want a perinatologist to do an obstetrical ultrasound with dopplers. I want to know how easily the blood is flowing."

"Okay," she conceded. "I'll go for that one, but not the amniocentesis or this PUBS thing you wrote here."

"That's a percutaneous umbilical blood sampling to test for genetic abnormalities or birth defects."

"No. I don't care and I don't want to know. I'll take them the way I get them."

"What if there's something that could be done now? That is my specialty you know. I'm getting pretty good at bringing spina bifida babies into the world practically unscathed."

"Michael, I know that. And don't think I don't appreciate all you're doing. But I personally feel that there's more to risk doing the test than not doing it. Especially with four babies. Can't we let God handle some of this?"

She heard his loud sigh over the phone before he said. "Yes, I guess we can. But get the new ultrasound done this week. Dr. Brarely is one of the best perinatologists around and you need to start seeing him soon anyway. He specializes in high-risk pregnancies, and in case no one has mentioned this to you, you are high-risk."

"Yes, sir!" she said with emphasis.

"And Shelley?"

"Yes?"

"Given any more thought to my suggestion?"

"The washcloths?" she asked in a confused voice.

He chuckled heartily. "No, not them. Marriage. To me."

"Oh. No. I didn't know I was supposed to be thinking about that. I thought we ironed all that out."

"Just asking again. Let me know if you change your mind."

"Okay. Hey, about those washcloths . . . ."

"Yeah?"

"Women don't really breast feed when they have this many babies, do they?"

"Yeah, they do. All the time. It's a commitment and it takes support, but it can be done. Women with quints have been known to successfully manage for better than a year."

"You're kidding!"

"No, I'm not. Really. Sure, it's frustrating at first, but once you get past the first few weeks and establish a schedule, it can be extremely rewarding, I promise."

"Why are you so gung-ho on this?"

"As a pediatrician, I think it is the single most important thing a mother can contribute other than love. Besides, I'm starting to have these wicked fantasies of watching you nurse," he chided.

"Yeah, like that's going to happen."

"It could."

"You know, at this point, I'm worried more about growing them than feeding them."

"As well you should be. By the way, I don't want you gaining any more than forty to fifty pounds."

"Forty to fifty pounds!"

"Don't protest too much, most women carrying quads usually gain ninety."

"Oh, Michael . . . what have I done?"

He chuckled into the phone. "I guess I'm partially to blame. I'm the one who insisted on you taking Pergonal."

"Yeah, well it worked real well didn't it?" she said sarcastically.

"Honey, anything I set my mind to, I do well. Real well. Hey, I gotta go, they're calling me down to surgery. Take care of yourself and tell Brarely to call me right away."

16 Weeks

THE BABIES ARE SIX INCHES IN LENGTH AND WEIGH ABOUT
FOUR OUNCES.

Gabby was on restriction up to the day before the Thanksgiving holiday because she had racked up close to $200 in roaming charges on her mom's cell phone calling Sam. Meanwhile, Sam, well aware that this long distance relationship didn't have a shot at getting off the ground unless they managed to see each other at least once a month, finally persuaded his father to let him go to his Aunt Shelley's for the four-day weekend. When Michele found out about Gabby being off of "groundation," just in time for Sam's last-minute flight to arrive, she knew this was somehow going to spell trouble for Mandy. And it did. Thursday, just hours after Sam had been picked up at the airport, he and Gabby disappeared for the day. They told Mandy that they were going to get a bus and walk around Chinatown. At four o'clock, when Michele still hadn't heard from either of them, she walked over to talk to Gabby's mother.

"I don't know what could be keeping them," said Gabby's mom, Denise. "They both knew that I was serving dinner at four and that I expected them back by 3:30 at the latest."

"Where could they be?" Michele asked as she paced back and forth in the over-warm kitchen.

Mandy was standing in the doorway, silently stewing because her cousin and her best friend had simply gone off and left her, but still feeling like she should try to take some heat off of them if she could. "I don't think either one of them was wearing a watch. Maybe they just lost track of time."

Michele walked over to where Mandy stood staring dejectedly at the floor and squeezed her shoulder. "I'm sure you're right. They probably just let the time get away from them."

When Gabby and Sam finally did show up, nobody was more surprised than them to discover how late it was. They had been walking and talking all afternoon and hadn't paid any attention to the time until the sun had started to set.

"We're really sorry, Aunt Shelley," Sam said. "We were just having such a good time. We must have walked close to ten miles. My calves are killing me. Aren't there any streets around here that don't have hills?"

Michele tousled his hair and smiled indulgently as she warmed a dinner plate for him. "Not very many, I'm afraid. Listen, I'm going to have to call your dad and ask him what I'm supposed to do about this. Gabby's mom is pretty shook up that you kept her out all day."

"Yeah, I know. She gave me a pretty dirty look when I dropped her off. Honestly, I didn't mean for Gabby to miss their Thanksgiving meal together."

"I know. But I can't have you being irresponsible like this and both of you really upset Amanda today. I'm sure she had no idea that you two planned to go off alone like that."

"Yeah, she did."

"What?"

"She's the reason we left when we did. She and Gabby got into a fight."

"Gabby and Amanda got into a fight?" The incredulity Sam heard in his aunt's voice emphasized how unusual that occurrence had been.

"Yeah. It was pretty bad."

"You're kidding."

"No, I'm not. If I hadn't heard her myself, I wouldn't have thought Manda capable of such cruel words."

"Just what did she say?"

"Aunt Shelley, I'd rather not say."

"Either you tell me, or we get on that phone right now and you tell your father."

"Sheesh okay. Okay . . . Manda accused Gabby of latching onto the first guy who looked cross-eyed at her, then she told Gabby not to be in such a big hurry to find a place where she and I could go to make out, because once I felt her up and screwed her, I'd just get right back on a plane and go home."

"Oh my God," Michele said as her hand went to cover her mouth. "I can't believe she would say something like that."

"Yeah, well, me neither. But she did. I was on the porch tying my shoes, and Gabby and Manda were in the hallway behind me."

"Why would she say something like that?"

"You got me. But that's one of the reasons Gabby didn't want to come back earlier. She said 'no way did she want to sit across a Thanksgiving table from her.'"

"I don't blame her! I'll go talk to Amanda right now and straighten her out!"

"Aunt Shelley, I wouldn't do that if I were you, at least not right now."

"Why not?"

"Well, the way I see it, Manda's probably getting just a little bit sick and tired of Gabby bringing me up all the time. She may even have a touch of jealousy because of it, and to top that off, I come in unexpectedly and sweep Gabby away. Well there's bound to be problems, they being so close and all, ya know?"

Michele smiled up at the lanky teenager. "You know, Sam, you've got to be one of the smartest men I've ever met. You figure that out all by yourself?"

"Well, you can't help but wonder when a nice kid like Manda goes off like that for nothing. It's these teenage hormones you know, too much estrogen, probably estradiol and not enough progesterone to balance it out."

Michele laughed as she placed the warmed-up dinner in front of him. "I'll take your word for it. You certainly know a whole lot more about that than I do."

Laying out new silverware and a fresh linen napkin for him, she added, "Okay, so now I know what's up with Mandy. Now, about you. Where'd you go to make out?"

He wolfed down a big glob of potatoes with a fork full of green beans. "I'm honor bound not to say. A gentleman doesn't disclose that kind of information."

"Well, Gabby's momma is probably grilling Gabby right now about what you two did together all day."

"And I would hope that Gabby will tell her nicely that it's none of her business, that we didn't do anything we shouldn't have."

"That isn't the way it's going to come down. If you want to see Gabby again, I highly recommend you find a way to give Mrs. Grissen a play by play that does not include any heavy petting."

"Now Aunt Shelley, what kind of louse do you think I am? You should know better than to think I'd compromise a girl. I may be only seventeen, but I know the way diseases get passed around and I definitely know how easy it is to get the reproductive cycle primed and receptive. I'm going to medical school. I don't have time for babies or syphilis, thank you very much."

"So you're saying you plan on abstaining until marriage?"

"Is that what you want to hear?"

"I'm pretty sure that's what Gabby's mother wants to hear right now."

"Then that's my story."

"I can't tell if you're just telling me what I want to hear, or if you're telling me the truth."

"Let's just say you and Mrs. Grissen don't have anything to worry about. Gabby knows her own mind and regardless of what I want, she has respect for herself. I know you think this thing between us is going too fast, but really, it's not. Gabby and I are going to be together for a very long time. We both know it and we don't care to rush things. But we also don't care to hear everybody telling us what to do. We're practically adults. At this point you can trust us."

Michele sat staring at this teenager who was more grown up then most men twice his age. "You're absolutely right, Sam. I couldn't agree with you more. Pie?"

"Yes indeed. This is good stuff. You're a good cook."

"Thank you, Sam."

"Dad says so, too."

"Does he?"

"Yeah, he talked for weeks about that dinner you fixed us. I think he misses you."

"Do you?" she asked with a tiny smile.

Sam grinned over at her and laughed. "Yeah, I do and I think you miss him, too." He wiped his mouth with a napkin and snickered, "I'd be more concerned with your improprieties than with mine, right now. You bein' the one expectin' without a husband."

Michele let out a big, long sigh. Then she tilted her head and stared at him quizzically. "Are you supposed to be working on me? Did he send you as a some kind of matrimonial delegation or something?"

"Nah. I just think you're good for each other. Same as it is with Gabby and me. Gotta run. Thanks for the grub. I told Gabby I'd come over and help her smooth things over with her mom and dad."

"Oh, well, now you've got your work cut out for you."

"No, not really. These days how many parents wouldn't jump at the chance to link their daughter up with a man who's going to be a surgeon?"

"You've got a point there, Sam, an excellent, excellent point. Go wow 'em. But be in by eleven."

"Eleven?"

"Eleven."

"Eleven-thirty," he said confidently.

"Eleven."

"Okay, eleven."

After finishing the dishes, Michele tromped up the stairs to confront Amanda. Oh, she did not like this part of motherhood. And she couldn't believe she was getting ready to start the whole cycle over again from the very beginning, with four more.

The rest of the holiday was uneventful. Gabby and Sam included Amanda in everything they did for the rest of the weekend, which made both Michele and Denise give a big sigh of relief. It was all too apparent to anyone who saw Gabby and Sam together that they were more than just smitten; they positively glowed in each other's presence.

When Michele took Sam back to the airport on Sunday night, a tearful Gabby accompanied them. Michele and Amanda gave them a few moments to be alone before watching Sam board at the gate. Watching surreptitiously as Sam and Gabby said good-bye, Michele was struck by the purity of their budding love. They were so considerate and sure of each other. You could see there was trust and faith in their future because they appeared to have it now. As Sam's towering frame crushed Gabby's slight one in a tight embrace, she sensed their restraint. Because there was complete devotion, they would never have to worry about those around them. She felt happy for them. Somehow she just knew that they'd make it.

On the way home, she listened as Gabby extolled Sam's virtues. If any man needed his own P.R. firm, Sam had it in Gabby. Between the two of them, they were going places and they'd be united doing it. She had to make sure Mandy understood that, because nothing was going to come between Sam and Gabby. Not now. And Mandy would just have to adjust to that fact. Gabby had a new best friend, not that she didn't still have a great friend in Mandy, but when you're in love, that friendship is the first and foremost; all others would be secondary to the prime source of their happiness. If this was true love, no one would ever be closer to them than they were to each other. Sometimes, more than anything, that was what she missed most about Kevin being gone. She missed having a true best friend almost as much as she missed having someone to love who could make the world spin just by being with her.

19 Weeks

THE BABIES CAN BE FELT BY THE MOTHER.

It was the week before Christmas when Michael and Sam arrived unexpectedly at Michele's house late one sunny afternoon. When they got to the glass-paneled front door, Michael could see Michele asleep on the love seat in the family room at the end of the long hallway.

Letting themselves in, they quietly set down their luggage, and while Sam went directly to the bathroom at the top of the stairs, Michael tiptoed into the family room.

Quietly, he pulled up a small ottoman and sat looking down at Michele as she slept. She was so beautiful it almost stopped his heart. Her soft lips were curved into a tiny bow-shaped smile, and her flushed cheeks were a mixture of pink and creamy white, her dark lashes lying over them were fluttering lightly with her even breathing.

How could something devastating be happening in this wonderful, nurturing body? But that was the reason he was here. Something about a test result had alarmed him. Alarmed him enough that he hadn't even bothered to call her before calling the airlines.

Suddenly her eyes fluttered open and she saw him. Her instant smile of recognition brightened her whole face. His world suddenly lit up and he couldn't understand why such a simple reaction on her part made him so happy.

Mandy came down the stairs with Sam behind her. He'd run into her upstairs and had immediately taken her aside in the hallway to ask if she would accompany him to the mall. He wanted her to help him find the perfect gift for Gabby. Mandy asked for permission and then grabbed a jacket from the hall closet before they left. As soon as the door closed behind them, it was evident to Michele that Michael had wanted to be alone with her.

"Hi," he whispered.

"Hi, yourself. What are you doing here?"

He watched her as she stretched languorously, allowing each small separation in her spine to get the full benefit of the motion.

"I came to check on you."

Something about the way he said that made her face scrunch in puzzlement.

"Why?" she asked pointedly, quirking one eyebrow as she tried to intimidate him into 'fessing up. Something was going on. He was pretending this was a spur-of-the-moment visit when it really wasn't.

Suddenly she was scared. She sat up and ran her hand through her hair. "Why have you come all this way? Dr. Brarely called you, didn't he? What's wrong? What's wrong with the babies? Was there something wrong with the Triple Screen Test?" She had gone from warm, soft, and fluid to alert, tense, and wary.

"Shh," he said gently as he eased her back down onto the couch. "It's probably nothing," he whispered, "I just need to check something."

"What?"

"Shelley, relax, it may be nothing. I'll know in a minute. I need to feel your womb. You need to trust me about this."

"What do you need to do?" she was terrified all of a sudden. Terrified for her babies.

"I need to insert my fingers into you and feel your womb, then while I'm doing that I need to press on your lower abdomen. And I need to listen to the heartbeats."

"Oh, Michael. What did Dr. Brarely tell you?"

"Just that he's worried. I only came to give a second opinion."

"I can't let you touch me that way," she said as she blushed full red.

"Not even clinically?" he asked smiling down at her, trying to ease her fears.

"It wouldn't be just clinical for me."

"Then I'll touch you intimately," he breathed huskily into the side of her neck.

"Don't be ridiculous, we've never even kissed."

"That's easily remedied," he said as his eyes met hers. Infinitesimally slowly, he lowered his head until his lips touched hers, and then something took over and he lost himself in the warm moistness of her mouth. His kiss became harsh as his passion was stoked like a blast furnace. Quick, hot flashes of hunger sped through him and suddenly, it wasn't enough just to taste her or press his lips against hers; he had to enter her and capture her, at least this part of her.

Hungrily his lips ravished her silkiness as he molded her lips to fit against his. And over and over again his tongue thrust its way inside, eager to explore, savor and possess. When her tongue finally, tentatively touched the underside of his, the moan that erupted from him shook them both to the core.

This was Michael who was kissing her. Michael, whose lips and tongue were so reminiscent of Kevin's, except that Kevin's kisses had never seemed this hot, this urgent, or this needy. And as experienced as Kevin's tongue had been, it had never made her nerve endings leap like tongues of fire in her mouth the way Michael's did.

Masking her own groan, she melted into his embrace and seared him back with her own quick, hot kisses, kisses with a passion equal to his. Her lips frantically lapped at his, her tongue darting around chasing his as his hands found her face and framed her mouth for one ravenous onslaught after another. Finally, when they were both breathing so erratically, that they couldn't quite catch their breath, he pulled away from her. Looking down into her flushed face, he used his most matter-of-fact doctor's voice and panted, "There, we've kissed. Now, take down your panties and part your legs for me."

It would have been the most incredibly erotic thing to hear if she hadn't remembered just then that the reason he wanted to "feel her up" was because he suspected something was wrong with the babies.

He was sitting on the edge of the sofa with his back to her and he felt her shift and dislodge him slightly as she self-consciously rearranged her clothes, trying to pull her skirt down with her hand. He thought she was doing his bidding, complying and getting ready for him, not refusing him. He took a small bottle and packet out of his jacket pocket and squirted a jellied liquid into his palm. Then he massaged it in before wiping his hands with the antiseptic wipe that he took from the small foil packet.

"Michael, I'm embarrassed . . . ."

"Don't be," he whispered. "Just pretend I'm any other doctor."

"I can't."

"Sure you can," he said as he pulled on a glove.

When he turned back he saw that she hadn't done anything more than move her bottom up off the back of her skirt and try to pull it down where it had ridden up while she'd been sleeping. So when she felt his fingers on the hem of her skirt and his hand slide up her thigh and then onto her hip, she gasped. Then before she could protest, with a crooked finger, he snagged the front waistband of her skimpy panties and dragged them down her legs. She heard the slight rustle of lace as her panties fell with a whispered sigh to the carpet. Then softer than she believed a man's hands had the right to be, she felt him part her thighs. Large hands moved up her inner thighs as he opened her wide for his inspection.

Not hesitating a second, for fear she'd fight him, he spread her labial lips with one hand and inserted the long middle finger from the other inside her vagina. He probed gently at first and then pressed more firmly up into her channel. His free hand lifted her skirt to her waist and then he gently began probing her flesh from the outside. His eyes were fixated on her face, watching as her blush deepened. His dark gray-blue eyes stared deeply into hers as he tried to calm her thoughts. Now he turned his face and with unfocused eyes he stared directly across the room at the opposite wall. He was concentrating on what he was feeling, his expression serious and troubled.

The hand on the inside was pressing up into her as the hand on the outside of her body was pressing down lightly to meet it. There were no tell-tale "hmmms" or "umms" emanating from his throat signifying a thoughtful doctor at work. But thoughtful he was as he felt all around her womb. Then he lifted her legs, bent at the knees, farther up toward her body as he tried to touch the rim of her cervix with his elongated digit.

He withdrew his finger and then his hand from where it was cupping her. Wordlessly, he closed her legs and put them down, then he stood and lifted her into his arms and carried her up to her bedroom where he laid her gingerly on the bed.

"I need to get my stethoscope and then I'm afraid I'm going to have to do a pelvic exam." The seriousness of the look on his face told her he'd brook no argument. There was something he had found, something was amiss.

So now, not only was she terrified for her babies, she was mortified that she was going to have to spread her legs wide and let Michael look into the most private part of her body. When his fingers had been inside her just now, it hadn't been so bad. Some aspects of him touching her had been quite wonderful in fact, despite the fear that had her wondering why he needed to do all this.

His professionalism was so ingrained that for all appearances, he had been detached. Even he believed that his fingers had only poked and prodded instead of stroked and caressed. Although for one moment, he hadn't actually been too sure about that. She had felt wet and slick and wonderful even through the glove, and as he tried to remember why his fingers were inside her, he had fought with himself to stay the clinical male. He had tried not to hurt her or shame her. A visual vaginal exam would be another matter all together. Christ! This was Shelley, his brother's wife! And he had kissed her. Oh, Lord, how he had kissed her! And she had kissed him back. He had no doubt that she had enjoyed his kisses.

When he returned from the living room with his bag a few moments later, she smiled up at him. This was Michael. Michael who cared about her, Michael who wouldn't let anything happen to her. Michael was family. But he was also a man, a damned handsome man who resembled Kevin in oh-so-many ways, but yet, was still so very different in his own right that she couldn't forget who he had once been to her. Once upon a time, he had been her teasing brother-in-law. Now, she had to force herself not to see him as the virile, attractive man that he was.

He sat on the edge of the bed close to her hip and gently pulled her skirt up past her expanding waist. He quirked his mouth slightly. It hadn't surprised him that she had managed to cover herself again while he was gone. Self-consciously, her hands flew to cover her mons venus. He did nothing more than pick them up, one by one, and place them off to her side. Then using a fully-opened hand he began to caress her lower abdomen with his slightly-cupped palm. Keeping his eyes on hers he rubbed her belly to relax her and, in turn, to relax the babies. After several moments, he placed a Pinard stethoscope, one used especially for hearing fetal heartbeats, just above her pubic region, then he bent forward and put his ear to it. He moved it slightly as he listened for a heartbeat and then he held it secure for several minutes before shifting it off to the right. Alternately, he listened to one side of her lower body then the other, then farther up and then farther back. Then he shifted her slightly onto her side and listened some more. She was shifted onto her other side while he listened, then he helped her to a semi-reclining position while he listened ever longer. Finally, he removed the stethoscope from her abdomen.

"I don't need to do the pelvic. I think I found out what I needed to know."

"What Michael? What? What's the matter with the babies?"

He gently pushed her back against the pillows and smoothed her skirt down to cover her. His eyes met hers and he reached for her hand. She thought she saw the glistening of a tear in his eye as he spoke softly with just a trace of hoarseness.

"I think we lost one, Shelley."

It took her a minute to absorb what he was telling her. And then she was confused. How had he known? And was it true? How could he know for sure? Oh God, one of her babies! No!

"No!" she screamed. "No!"

"Yes, honey. I think so."

"Why? Why do you think so?" she moaned through her sobbing.

He came up to sit with her at the head of the bed, both of them leaning back against the headboard. He wrapped his arm around her shoulders and pulled her close, snuggling her under it.

"When Dr. Brarely told me he wasn't sure he was getting four distinctive heartbeats, I got worried. Then when the sonogram consistently only showed three, I found it hard to believe that the other one was simply hiding. But when I felt your womb, I had to agree with Dr. Brarely, you're not stretching enough to accommodate four babies. You're hardly growing enough to handle three. We may even need you to take something to make your womb relax and become more elastic, it's not thinning as well as it should be. It's a tough muscle and yours is adamant that it wants to stay high and tight instead of loose and welcoming."

"Oh, Michael. So what do we do now?"

"We give you something to relax it a little and to make sure you're not contracting those muscles and making things too tight for the babies. Then we wait."

"What about the baby that died? Don't we have to take it out? Won't it make the others sick?"

"No. Not at this early stage of gestation. It will just shrivel and wilt and most of it will become reabsorbed back into the body. There's nothing toxic at this point to affect the others unless the cord tears something and makes you bleed." Seeing her blanch, he quickly added, "But I don't think that's going to happen. That's a rarity. I think everything will be fine once we get you to loosen up a bit."

He swung his legs over the side of the bed and picked up the phone. He punched in a series of numbers and she listened as she heard him talking to someone. Within a few minutes, she realized that he was talking to Sam. "Yeah, the one on Travis Avenue. I'll call it in, you pick it up on your way home. No. Yes. Yes, I think so. Don't dawdle, but don't hurry either. I think we need a few more minutes alone."

Then she heard him disconnect and dial another number. She heard him talking to what she assumed was a pharmacist, giving very detailed instructions as to brand and milligrams. "Okay, give me two of what you have on hand for tonight, but tomorrow get me the real deal, enough for twice a day for three weeks. Thanks. My son has my physician's card with him. If there's any problem, you can call my office in Denver for substantiation. Yes, Yes. Thank you."

"I take it you've decided to stretch my muscles," she said with a tiny smile.

"Got to. You're crowding my babies. I can't have that."

He resettled himself beside her and tucked her under the crook of his arm. Softly he stroked her cheek and then the side of her neck. "Are you okay?"

"Yeah. I just wanted them all. I don't know why. I was stunned when I learned that there were four and I had no idea how I'd manage, but then I wanted each and every one."

"I know," he said as he continued to stroke the inside of her elbow and arm.

"Why did it die?" she asked softly.

"Honey, there's no sure way to know. It could be any number of things. Unfortunately, with multiple births, the odds for problems are greatly increased. I suspect it had more to do the placement of the placenta than anything else. But it could just as easily have been an implantation problem."

"So it's nothing I could have done?"

He gathered her up closer. "No sweetheart," he whispered into the side of her neck. "Please believe me, it wasn't your fault. You didn't do anything wrong and there's nothing you could have done to prevent it. These things just happen. The other three will have a much better chance now." He continued to stroke his fingers up and down her arm and massaged her neck with infinite tenderness.

After a few moments of his easy, gentle touch, it didn't seem at all strange when he gingerly lifted her skirt and rubbed his large hand over her rounded belly.

He was still holding her and caressing her tummy when they heard the kids come in the front door twenty minutes later. Michael pushed her skirt down, placed his foot on the floor, and bent over to retrieve her panties for her. Thankfully, he had remembered to pick them up on his way back upstairs when he'd gone down for his bag.

"It's going to be a shame to have to shave off all those soft auburn curls," he said with a smile as he stood up and went to stand in front of the dresser mirror. He was using his fingers to comb his hair back into place and he was smiling into the mirror at her lying on the bed struggling into her panties behind him.

She was blushing big time now. "What are you talking about? Why do I have to be shaved?"

"Dr. Brarely has told you that you're delivering by C-section hasn't he?"

"No. No, he hasn't!"

"Oh shit."

"Michael!"

"Forget it. We'll talk about this later."

"The hell we will! What are you talking about?"

"Shelley," he said as he held her arms in his large hands. "First of all, there's the timing here, you know all about that. There are two teams of doctors that have to be ready at the exact same time."

"Yeah, so? That doesn't preclude vaginal delivery."

"It's better, for both you and the babies. And the cords." He was grasping at straws here and she knew it. His mind went back to the day, just a few weeks ago, when he'd finally received a copy of her medical files. He wished he had known how difficult her first delivery had been before consenting to donate his sperm to impregnate her again. Had he known, he probably would have refused her.

"Michael, what are you not telling me?"

"Nothing, it's just mostly standard procedure with multiple births like this."

"Michael . . . ."

"Okay, okay. You cannot be awake for this."

"Why the hell not?"

He turned around and faced out the window. After a few moments of silence, he finally let out a big sigh and turned back to face her. "Because . . . because there's so much that can go wrong and both Dr. Brarely and I believe that you're too small. You had a real hard time with Amanda because of that, and she wasn't a big baby. You had to have a transfusion for Chrissake! It's not wise to take this kind of chance when there's more than one baby to consider. It would be better for all the babies, if at the first sign of distress, we were ready to take them."

"When did you become the expert here? This isn't even your specialty!"

"I'm making it my specialty! Dr. Brarely and I have talked and I've decided that I'm going to be the delivering doctor."

"Oh you have, have you? Is that what this is all about? What if I don't want you there? Don't I have a say in this?"

"Why wouldn't you want me there?" he asked, his voice suddenly soft with a trace of hurt showing.

She shrugged her shoulders and shook her head, not at all sure how she could tell him about a woman's desire to only look her best in front of the man she was becoming somewhat attracted to. How embarrassing this would be for her. Huge of girth, swollen beyond endurance, gasping and trembling with pain, and spread open in ways both humiliating and humbling, these were not the ways she wished Michael to see her.

"I'm reading everything I can about both procedures, and I'm standing in on all C-section multiple deliveries back in Denver whenever I can get there."

"So that's why you want to cut me up the middle instead of letting me deliver vaginally?" she asked, the incredulousness of the statement ringing in her ears. "Because that's what you're relearning?"

"No. Of course not! As the delivering doctor, I deem it as the safest way to deliver these babies. We're not taking any unnecessary chances this way. Besides, there have been many strides in C-sections in the last years. The cut is not up the middle anymore, it's shorter and totally different, the muscles aren't cut like they used to be. They're pushed aside and the healing time is faster, the scarring minimal. And one day when you remarry, you'll still have tone and elasticity in your vaginal walls. Your future husband will thank me!"

"No. I hear all your reasons, but I know you. You're thinking of me. Damn it, admit it Michael! You're trying to protect me, not the babies!"

"Well, yeah, you are the mother. Where will the babies be, where will Mandy be if something happens to you?"

"Nothing is going to happen to me."

"Michele," he said as he came to stand beside her. "Don't be stalwart on this, take the sure way, the tried and true way. Let's not leave anything more to chance than we have to, please? You're too tiny. I've already felt you for Christ sake! And you nearly died delivering Amanda!"

She looked up into his face and saw the sincerity there, and something else. Was that fear?

"You're right, we have lots of time later to talk about this. It's a debate I don't think I can win tonight."

"It's a debate you can't win on any given night. I'm afraid of losing you, Michele. I'm going to insist we opt for the safest delivery possible. What the hell would I do with three babies on top of the two children we already have if anything happened to you?"

Three babies. Just yesterday, it had been four. Or so she'd thought. She wondered for a moment how long ago it was that her baby had died.

They heard the kids in the kitchen and they linked hands. "Just promise me this isn't a done deal. I need to feel I have some say about these things. After all, it is my body."

"And a fine body it is, too," he said with a small pat on her rump as he led her out of the room.

Michael went directly to the bag Sam had put on the counter, tore it open, and took out the vial. After examining it carefully, he took out one tiny pill and took it together with a glass of water over to Michele. "Here, time for your medicine." He leaned in close to her and whispered in her ear, "I want you to give my kids a little more elbow room down there."

She smiled up at him and took the pill out of his hand. "As long as we're not talking the size of a football field or anything."

"Nah, maybe just big enough for a small hockey rink."

"They're girls. All girls."

"Boys. All boys."

Mandy, Gabby, and Sam were looking over at them shaking their heads. The adults were getting more like children every day.

Mandy had to turn away to hide the hurt that was showing in her eyes. Her mother looked so happy right now, she didn't even seem to know that Mandy existed anymore. She hadn't even noticed that she'd had a huge henna tattoo installed on her midriff two days ago. And Gabby and Sam were in a world of their own. Even when she was with them, she felt alone.

The five of them enjoyed a big carry-in pizza dinner and then Michael and Sam left in their rental car to go back to the airport. Michael had received an emergency page. Instead of staying the night as they'd planned, he had to rush back to Denver. Just before they left, Michael took Michele aside and held both her hands.

"I want you to know we're in this together. You carry the babies and take care of yourself. Then when it's time, I'll do my part and make sure they enter this world safe and sound. Trust me, Shelley. Trust me to take care of you and the babies." He was looking down into her face, his eyes reflecting slate blue by the porch light. He let go of one of her hands and caressed the side of her cheek as he smiled down at her.

"I do, Michael. This is just all so new to me."

"I know. But remember, I'm here for you. All you need to do is call me. I can be here in a matter of hours. If you're scared or worried about anything, please call me."

"I will."

He bent down and touched her lips lightly with his. It was a sweet parting kiss, one that could have said all manner of things. But since the kids were watching, it was saying, family-saying-good-bye-to-family, instead of what it really was—one incredibly turned on man saying good-bye to one shy little temptress who was totally unaware of the web she was spinning around him.

Michele, Amanda, and Gabby stood on the front porch waving until they were gone and then Michele turned to Gabby and said, "You need to go home now, sweetheart. Mandy and I need to talk about this tattoo she's plastered all over her body."

Both girls' eyes went wide with shock as they turned toward each other. Gabby looked at Amanda with sympathy as she slowly backed down the porch steps.

"Uh, yeah, right. I guess I'll go then. See ya tomorrow Mandy."

Michele waited until Mandy waved good-bye and then followed her into the house. "Did you not think I'd find out?"

"How did you, anyway?"

"When you reached up into the top oven to get the garlic bread out, your shirt came away from your jeans. Imagine my surprise to see a big purple and brown tattoo. What's it of?"

"A big butterfly."

"How long until it wears off?"

"A month or so."

"How 'bout we hurry it up some with a Brillo?"

"Mom!"

"Okay, okay. Just use the loofah, twice a day. But this isn't over. You've got to be punished for this. You knew I wouldn't approve. Who did it anyway?"

"The guy who runs the little jewelry kiosk at the mall."

"You let a guy touch you there?"

"Yes, Mom. That's how it's done. You go lay on a table and he puts it on."

"Show me the whole thing," she demanded.

Mandy lifted her shirt and Michele started at the hideous blob of sepia tones that was supposed to be a henna-colored butterfly. Her eyes were wide and her face flushed with anger. Parts of the butterfly were clearly well below her navel.

"Did you remove all your clothes for this?"

"No, I just pulled them out of the way."

"Your jeans, too?"

"I just had to unzip them a little. Jeremy was very proper about it all."

"Jeremy. This Jeremy had you naked from the bottom of your bra to just above your pubic region. Pray tell, where did this all take place?"

"I told you, at the mall. At the jewelry kiosk."

"In the center of the mall where anybody could watch?"

"Yeah, that's the cool part, all your friends egging you on and oohing and ahhing over the whole thing."

Michele shook her head. "I cannot believe this. I've raised you better than this. I simply cannot believe you did this, nevertheless in a public place where everybody could watch."

"Everybody's doing it, Mom. It's no big deal."

"It's a big deal to me!"

"Well you're way behind the times. Way behind the times."

"And just how much did this, this . . . butterfly cost?"

"Sixty dollars."

"Sixty dollars!"

"It's my money. It came from my birthday money. And I'm happy about it!"

"Well I'm not! And that's all that matters!"

"Why is that? Why is it only what you want that matters? Why do you always get things your way and I never get mine? Why is that, do you think?"

Mandy was screaming now, and Michele was watching her wide-eyed as her daughter broke down and started sobbing.

"Why do you get to have babies and people fawning all over you while I get diddly? I don't even get to have a boy-friend like Gabby. Pretty soon my hair will start falling out again, and I'll be skin and bones while Gabby's growing taller and getting even bigger boobs. And don't think Sam doesn't notice. I saw him ogling her all day!"

Oh, so that's what this was all about. This was not about being rebellious and getting a tattoo to tick off Mom. This was Mandy being afraid of what she knew was coming, Mandy not being the center of attention because of the babies, Mandy afraid of losing her best friend to a boy, and boys that weren't giving her a second glance right now because she was pale and skinny with short, wispy, thinning hair and a mysterious illness that scared the hell out of them.

She opened her arms and Mandy flew into them. And there in the kitchen Michele held her close and rocked her back and forth, stroking her hands along her back. "Shhh. Shhh. It's okay. Everything's going to be okay. You'll see. One of your brothers or sisters will be here soon to help you out. And then you'll get all better. Your hair will grow back in, you'll get all your curves back again, and you'll have boobs to beat the band! You'll see. The boys will be tripping over themselves trying to get to you."

Michele held Mandy at arm's length and wiped at her tears as she tried to get Mandy to smile. "In fact, I hear that the boob gene is inherited from your mother, and I'm not too shabby in that department," Michele said as she shoved her shoulders back and showcased her 38Cs. They were actually more like 38Ds right now because of the babies, but Mandy didn't know that.

Mandy sniffled but she managed a smile for her mom. "Yeah, I'll show her. Her mom's not much in the boob department."

Michele hugged her tight to her chest and whispered, "Everything's going to be all right, baby. Just wait and see. Everything's going to be good again. Real soon."

"Do you really think so, Mom?"

"I know so. Now get up there and get a shower and try not to use any soap on that tattoo."

When Mandy stopped and turned to stare at her, she added with a smile, "Might as well make it last for all it cost you in money and modesty."

Mandy smiled back at her and continued on down the hallway to the stairs.

Michele slumped into the nearest chair. *Dear God, I sure hope this works. I just can't stand losing her if it doesn't.*

That night after Mandy's shower, they sat together on the sofa while Michele showed Mandy some computer printouts and some articles she'd copied from some library books.

"It says here that the babies are going to be peeing inside you," Mandy said.

"Well, yes, I suppose that they will be," Michele said with a smile as she stroked Mandy's hair. "In fact, you were rushed away from me right after you were delivered because the doctor saw some meconium in the bag of waters."

"Meconium?"

"Yeah. In the last few weeks the baby's first bowel movement collects in the bowel, and sometimes, they just can't hold it all in. Sometimes, some of it finds its way into their mouth and they aspirate it into their lungs. It can be a serious problem because it's like tar and very sticky, hard to get up and out."

"That is so gross!"

Michele smiled at her. "Yeah, actually the whole process is pretty gross. I like the stork story much better. Sometimes, I wish it really happened that way."

"So, you really think this will work, Mom?" The sudden sincerity in Mandy's face told Michele that Mandy was afraid to place too much hope on a miracle happening for her.

"Yeah. And so do Michael and Sam. And you know if Sam is all for it, then it's practically a guarantee. He's the one who's done most of the research for me."

"Just what is a stem cell?"

"It's just a blob of life, tissue that has the potential to grow into blood, bone, or brain matter. Stem cells are nothing more than immature cells produced in bone marrow. They can divide to make more stem cells, which can develop into red or white blood cells and platelets. Stem cells are also derived from placentas, since the placenta is a vascular organ, but the umbilical cord has the rich, rich, richest blood cells. And that's what we want for my girl," Michele said. "We want the best, best, bestest for you," she said as she rumpled Mandy's nightgown, tickling her.

When they had both settled down from their hooting and hollering, Mandy looked over at her mom and smiled. "I think you're crazy to be doing all this for me, but thanks. I hope it works."

Michele looked over at her daughter and smiled. "It'll work baby, it'll work. Now go to bed, you have school tomorrow."

She listened as Mandy climbed the steps, her eyes focused on a picture of an unborn baby on one of the research papers she'd put on the coffee table in front of her. *It has to work,* she told herself. *It just has to.*

The next day Michele called Michael to tell him she thought she felt one of the babies move. It had been a flutter similar to the ones she'd had with Amanda, only she had felt it a lot lower than she had ever felt one of Amanda's kicks.

Michael was both pleased and unsettled to hear that she'd experienced the quickening of one of the babies. Selfishly, he wanted to caress her smooth belly and feel it, too.

"So are you using the Turkish washcloths?"

"Are you asking me if I'm pinching, pulling, and polishing my nipples as instructed?"

He chuckled. "Indeed I am. So are you doing the three P's as I recommended?"

"Yes, Michael. Whenever I'm in the shower. However, there is a slight problem there."

"Yeah, what's that?"

"It makes my tummy hard and I feel a funny tightening all around my lower abdomen. Like a belt tightening and loosening, only lower than my waist."

"Uh oh. That's not so good. Those are contractions. Well, actually, it's good and bad."

"Which is it Michael?"

"It's good that you're so sexually responsive, but it's bad that the connection from your nipples is causing these minor contractions."

"Is that what they are?"

"Yes, they're similar to Braxton-Hicks contractions, only you're causing them yourself."

"Exactly how am I doing that?"

"That's what I would like to know. Next time try to figure out which of the P's is causing them. Then let me know. And don't do that one anymore."

"Why?"

"Well, the one thing we certainly don't need is premature labor. So whichever one is causing that effect, you'll have to discontinue doing it."

"So why do *you* need to know which one it is?"

Because that's the one that is giving you sexual pleasure, and I think I could use that knowledge someday, he said to himself. To her he said, "Just as a heads-up on your conditioning process. If you can't use the washcloths, I'll send you some special cream."

"Why is this happening? What causes it?"

"Most women have a direct connection from their nipples to their womb. A baby nursing causes the womb to tighten and pull back into itself after delivery, but each woman is different. They respond differently to each type of stimulation. If your uterus is contracting when you pull on your nipples, then that's the stimuli that lubricates and readies you for sex as well. Sexual activity may release oxytocin, a hormone that stimulates uterine contractions."

"And that causes premature labor?"

"Yes. In fact, oxytocin is one of the drugs we administer to bring on labor."

"And I release it into my body when I touch my nipples in a certain way?"

"Apparently. You probably always have had the tightening, you just never felt it in the same way. When you're not pregnant or nursing, the foreplay caused by stimulating your nipples manifests itself as a heavy ache, making you welcoming and wet and desirous of penetration. The heavy feeling comes from the nipples signaling blood to flow into the area. It's your body's way of getting your womb ready for conception."

"It's the pinching. It's definitely the pinching," she said as she uttered a deep sigh.

Michael almost fell out of his seat. "H-how do you know?"

"I've been testing the ways while we've been talking. It is most definitely the pinching."

"Well stop!" he said harshly. Almost too harshly. She was driving him absolutely crazy. He was picturing her with her hand under her shirt, her bra pulled aside and her fingers caressing and pinching her own nipples. Surely they would be swollen and large now, extended abnormally from pregnancy hormones. He groaned out loud at the thought.

"Michael? Are you okay?"

"Yeah. I just . . . I just . . . I just have to go now. I dropped some files on the floor," he improvised.

"Okay, I'll talk to you later. Make sure you get everything in the right folder. It wouldn't do to get your patients all screwed up."

All screwed up? God he wished she was here and he was screwing *her* all up. Up, down, sideways. He just wished he was screwing her. "Go eat an apple," he muttered and then disconnected the line. When he looked down at himself he wasn't surprised to see the large bulge in his slacks reaching for the ceiling. God, what she did to him. He was hornier than a toad.

20 Weeks

RHYTHMIC MOVEMENTS IN THE ABDOMEN CAN MEAN A BABY HAS
THE HICCUPS.

S am opened the studio card that Gabby had sent him. Somehow they had gotten into the habit of exchanging romantic
greeting cards. Today's showed the back of a man and a woman
walking on the beach hand-in-hand looking into each other's eyes.
Inside it said, "I only have eyes for you." "And everything else I have
is for you, too," Gabby had added.

Drawn in the body of the card was a caricature of her with a
hound dog expression with tears running down one cheek.
Underneath it said, "I miss you."

He missed her, too. They talked on the phone practically
every day but it wasn't the same as being there, with her, in the
same room. Watching her smile up at him, feeling her hands go
around his neck as she pulled him down for a kiss.

He felt closer to Gabby than he had ever felt to anyone in his
whole life. Sure, he had been close to his mom, but that was
different; that was basking in affection from a mother's love,
enjoying the protection and devotion of one who could see nothing wrong with the child she had created and nurtured. With his
dad, it was like living in a college dorm one week and running

sports marathons the next. They studied hard, worked until they were exhausted, and then regrouped to play just as hard. They ran around like playboys on the slopes, intent on besting any daring oncomers while greedily satisfying the tension in their athletic bodies and feeding their hunger for competition. He couldn't wait to get Gabby out on the slopes. He wanted to show her how accomplished he was as a skier. He wanted to prove to her he was manly, proficient, and powerful. But mostly, he wanted to hold her and urge her to touch him. Touch him in intimate places. He wanted to take her to a remote slope he knew about where a deserted ranger station waited, and show her what thoughts of her did to him. He wanted her exclusively, and as the card said, he wanted to avail himself of the "everything else I have is yours, too." He was full blown in love and couldn't stand dealing with the distance they had between them.

Rashly, he pulled a card out of the drug store bag and started writing.

The front of the card had a picture of a beautiful bride on it. The header at the top said, "When she asked me what kind of wedding I wanted, I said, 'The one that makes you mine.'"

Inside, he scrawled, "Gabby, will you do me the honor of becoming my wife on June 24, 2012? I will be a doctor then and able to support us. I love you and don't want to even consider going on without a promise from you that will be forever mine. Love, Sam."

"P.S. If you say 'Yes,' I'll get a ring. I have money in savings, just let me know your size."

Before he could change his mind, he addressed the envelope and drove to the post office.

21 Weeks

LANUGO, A SOFT, DOWNY HAIR IS BEING REPLACED BY THICKER HAIR.

Christmas week was a little lonely for everybody. Michael couldn't take any time off from work because he had scheduled surgeries and consultations with families who needed to travel across the country to see him. Most doctors take the holidays as vacation time, but Michael tried to accommodate his patients by seeing that the children missed the least amount of school time possible. So the last weeks of December were, by far, his busiest throughout the year.

Sam had scheduled college entrance exams and was interviewing at his father's alma mater so he couldn't arrange to see Gabby. But Gabby, having received Sam's proposal in the mail, was still on cloud nine. They had decided not to tell anyone, but Gabby just had to tell Mandy.

Mandy was finally getting used to the idea of the babies and was actually getting a little involved with shopping for baby presents for her siblings. This was the last Christmas she would have her mother all to herself, and since she was feeling much better than she had last year, she was up for all the traditional baking she and her mom had missed out on last year. Her grandmother was still cruising the Mediterranean but she had sent a card with a picture of a classic mustang on it, hinting that there might just be one similar to that in her future, if she kept her grades up and her mother approved. So . . . studying was definitely in the works for the holiday break.

Michele was really starting to show and was fielding questions whenever she went out. It was only a matter of time before her mother got the word, so she promised herself that over the holidays, she would take the time to pen a long letter explaining everything. She was looking forward to doing all the things she and Mandy had missed out on last year because Mandy had been in the hospital at Christmas time. She spent hours shopping for Mandy, Gabby, Michael, and Sam, and of course, for the babies. And everywhere she went, she saw sweet maternity clothes that she just had to have, so Santa brought her a whole new wardrobe on Christmas day.

22 Weeks

THE BABIES ARE ABOUT ONE POUND AND ALMOST HALF THE LENGTH
THEY WILL BE AT BIRTH.

There was a small rust-colored stain in the middle of her underwear. As her eyes focused on it, she tried to envision what it could mean. Nothing good, for sure. It was Sunday morning, the last day of the long New Year holiday, and she knew it would be hard to get Dr. Brarely. She'd have to call his service and wait until they found him, and it probably wasn't all that crucial. After debating for a few minutes, she decided to call Michael in Denver. She knew he played racquetball on Sunday mornings but she had his pager number. It was early. Maybe he hadn't left yet, she mused, as she punched in his number. His service forwarded her page to his cell phone and a connection was finally made.

When he answered the phone, he was all businesslike until he recognized her voice.

"Hi, babe. What's up?"

"Michael, I had some staining about half an hour ago."

"What color?" he asked brusquely.

"Brown, I guess. With reddish brown flecks in it."

"Damn! That's not good. Shelley, get off the phone and call for an ambulance. You need to get to the hospital right away. I'll call ahead then get to the airport. I'll get there as soon as I can."

"What's happening Michael?" she asked with terror in her voice.

"One of the babies is apparently in distress. Just do as I say and get to the hospital as soon as possible and don't drive yourself. Don't lift anything either!"

As soon as Michael hung up, he put in a call to the emergency room in San Francisco. Then he called a friend he knew in the corporate world and arranged to borrow his pilot and jet.

Three hours later, he was conferring with Shelley's doctors as he looked over her latest test results. Her blood count was way too low. He had been met by a surgeon as soon as he'd arrived at the hospital and now he was frantically paging through her chart as the other doctors watched him.

Everyone knew Michele was his sister-in-law and that the babies she carried were his through insemination. Still, they deferred to his renowned status, mindful that since he was one of the best pediatric surgeons in the country, he was the one in charge, even though he had an emotional connection to the patient.

The fetal heartbeat for the baby in question was negligible. The results were not good and he knew it. They had given her a combination of tocolytics to delay contractions, but her body had already started the process of trying to pass the baby. And if one went, the others could just as easily follow. Dr. Brarely was reviewing ultrasound pictures on a computer on the other side of the room.

"Your hunch was right Michael. It looks like placenta previa, low-lying and practically complete. It isn't safe to use a vaginal probe, so we don't have all the information we could use here, but it's pretty obvious what needs to be done. Are you going to do the surgery or am I?"

"I'll do it, but I just can't let her wake up to find out she's lost one of her babies. I have to prepare her for the worst before she's prepped."

He ran his fingers through his hair and sighed long and loud. "Because of her history I'm very worried about a post-partum hemorrhage. I'm especially worried about an accreta. If she has the complication of an accreta and we have to resort to surgery to get the placenta to release, we might have to perform a hysterectomy to keep her alive." He directed his eyes to one of the other doctors. "Dan, make damned sure we have all the blood we could possibly need for transfusion." His eyes flew to another one of the team members. "Bob, I want you to assist. Brarely, if you wouldn't mind, I could use you in there to second guess me and to lend an extra hand or two if it gets dicey. I'll be right back to wash up." He strode out of the surgical wing to go see Shelley in the emergency labor area.

Her normally pale skin looked even paler against the pastel gown and the white of the sheets. She was hooked up to an IV and a fetal heart monitor. He walked briskly into the room and took her hand in his. Her eyes flew open and she smiled up at him. He forced himself to smile back and reached to brush a wisp of hair back from her forehead.

Knowing that he didn't have the time to sugar coat this, he started right in. "One of the babies' placentas has pulled away from the wall of the uterus. It's called placenta previa. It's a condition where the placenta is located too close to the opening of the uterus. It can cause the baby to lie in the uterus sideways or breech. It occurs in one out of every 250 pregnancies, so it's pretty common, especially in multiple births. The condition can be complete, partial, marginal, or low-lying. Unfortunately, we believe yours is complete. The cord is barely pulsing, the amniotic fluid level is hardly discernible and you now have a significant amount of vaginal bleeding. We have to go in and it doesn't look good." He took a big breath to steady himself.

"Shelley, a complete placenta previa must be removed to stop a life-threatening hemorrhage. Which means you would lose the baby. At this time, the other two seem fine, but anything can happen with this kind of thing. I'll try to fix the cord, but it may already be too late."

"Oh, God."

"I wanted you to know how serious this was before they put you under."

"Michael, don't let them take my babies!"

"I'm more concerned for your welfare than that of the babies' right now, but you know, I already love those babies."

"Michael, please. Don't let them take the babies!"

"Shelley, I'm not going to let you hemorrhage. If there's a chance you aren't going to make it, I'm sorry, but I can't let that happen."

"Save our babies, Michael."

"Shelley," he said as he bent low to kiss her on the cheek. "You know that I will do everything I can after I'm sure that you're taken care of. The babies come after you, no matter what. They are my second concern, you are my first. But don't ever doubt how important the babies are to me, don't ever doubt it," he whispered against her cheek.

"This is Dr. Zeng. He's going to get you ready. You have to go under general anesthesia now, but I had to let you know what we're up against before we operated."

"Michael, please . . . ."

"Sweetheart, just try to relax and let me and the other doctors do what we're trained for. These are my babies, too."

"Amanda . . . . What about Amanda? The cord . . . ."

"We can't worry about Amanda right now, Shell. Trust me, if there's anything I can do, I will . . . for you, for the babies, and for Amanda, but most importantly right now, for you. You're going to be fine. We'll deal with whatever comes later. I'll see you soon," he said as the other doctor moved to put the gas mask over her face.

"I'm scared."

"Don't be. I'll be taking care of you. Go to sleep now. I'll be here when you wake up." She thought she heard him say *I love you Michele*, but she couldn't be sure, the hiss of gas escaping was loud in her ears. Then everything went black.

Many hours later, a very tired Michael sat beside Michele's bed, her small hand firmly enclosed in his as he dozed in the chair. Somehow he knew when her eyes opened and she tried to force them to focus. Coming up through the fog, she had only one desperate question in her eyes, and he dreaded answering it. But he had to.

"We couldn't save the baby. The cord had been compromised too long."

"And the others?" she asked through dry, cracked lips.

He held a straw for her as he encouraged her to drink some water from a cup on the side table.

"They're fine. A boy and a girl. I touched them both," he said with a big grin.

"Was it a girl or a boy?"

"A girl."

"And the cord?"

"They're working with it now, trying to harvest what they can. It was barely pulsing when we took it. It may not be viable. There are very few stem cells found in cord blood. That's why this procedure is only used to treat children. Since Mandy is so underweight and pretty tiny normally, they may get enough. It's hard to tell. The embryonic stem cells could all be dead by now. The cords are usually two feet long or better at delivery. This one was barely six inches. We won't know for a few more hours if it'll do the trick. Amanda's being prepped, just in case. And since this was all so unexpected, there may only be time for one or two chemo treatments. They like to follow that up with radiation to ensure that they've destroyed the bone marrow. But in this case, it's not advised. Just in case it doesn't work, she'll still be able to wait for the next one. But on the plus side, even though this will be an allogeneic transplant, it could still work."

"Allogeneic?"

"Not from a twin. Cells from a twin would be a shoo in, but it is her sister's. So at least chances for graft versus host disease or rejection are minimal."

"Oh my poor baby."

"Which one?" he asked.

"Both," she said simply, her eyes filling with tears.

He squeezed her hand and then brought it to his lips. "You scared me. Don't do that anymore."

They went ahead with the transplant of the cells they could save even though there wasn't the great hope that there should have been. The field being too new, everything was uncertain at best. There were some cells still dividing in the center of the cord, some cells that couldn't hurt, only help, but it was doubtful that there was enough there to work with.

Michele was very upset that she couldn't be with Amanda while they infused the cells though a catheter in Mandy's chest, just two floors down. But because Mandy was given immune-suppressing chemotherapy in preparation for the transplant, she was in isolation. Michael went down to see Mandy, to hold her hand and to explain everything they were doing to her. Then they all prayed that the stem cells traveling to the bone marrow did their job and multiplied like crazy.

The next day, Michele insisted on arranging for the baby's funeral from her hospital bed.

"I'm glad I had already picked out some names. Martin, Marci, and Melissa. I want to name her Marci. Of all the names, that one was my favorite."

"Why pick the name that's your favorite? Then you won't be able to use it for one of the others."

"I can't give her much, Michael. But I can at least give her a name that I love. A name that will always be very special to me. She will always have a special place in my heart. I'm so sorry I couldn't keep her."

"It wasn't anything you did or didn't do. The placenta was just in the wrong place, through absolutely no fault of your own."

"I know. But as her mother, I'll always wish that things had happened differently."

He took her hand and pressed a kiss into the palm. "Marci, it is. Baby Marci Moore, sister to Amanda."

"Yes, that would be nice for her stone."

"She needs a stone, too?"

"Yes. Please?"

He bent down and kissed her on the cheek. "Whatever you say. For some reason, I'm not able to say no to you anymore," he said as he wiped a tear from her eye.

He left her to go check on Amanda, thinking as he went that Michele was quite an unusual woman. Most women wouldn't waste a name that they loved for a baby they had to bury as a stillborn. They'd save the name and use it for one that lived. But not Michele, she wanted Marci to have a name of honor. A name she loved as truly as she'd loved her. Then it occurred to him that all the names began with an 'M.' Marci, Martin, Melissa. Michele and Michael. Just what was the significance to that, if any, he wondered. He'd have to remember to ask Michele about that.

The day after Marci was buried, Michael approached Michele about the idea of moving to Denver. She was still in the hospital recovering and so was Amanda.

"Just until the babies are born. Then you can move back if you want. Right now, I think you need to be where I can keep an eye on you. You will receive excellent care there. We have one of the best facilities for handling difficult pregnancies in the country."

"So does San Francisco."

"Yes, but they don't have me. I need you to be there. I need to work and I can't do it if I'm continually worried about you and the twins."

The twins. They had gone from quads, to triplets, and now to twins. Even if the cord they had used performed the prayed-for miracle and Mandy recovered completely, Michele knew that if she lost the remaining babies, both she and Michael would be completely devastated. Somehow, they had become deeply attached to them and now they were more important than either cared to say.

"I don't want to move. Anyway, I don't have the time or the energy to orchestrate all that. And I love San Francisco."

"You don't have to actually move. Just bring what you'll need and we'll close up the house until you return. You won't need to bring anything but your clothes, and not very many of those. Anything you need you can find in Denver."

"What about Amanda? She has school, her doctors, Gabby."

"Amanda can finish this year out at the same high school Sam attends. She's not in any treatment program right now, she's just waiting for the cord cell transplant to take, and it would actually be better if she were in Denver anyway. Dr. Kensible is the leading researcher in the field and he lives just outside of Denver. He's a good friend of mine. I beat him in racquetball on a regular basis. Gabby . . . well, Gabby can come visit anytime she wants. Though the way she and Sam are right now, I think they could both use a nice long separation. It sounds like they're getting way too serious. And anyway, Mandy and Gabby's friendship is being strained by Sam."

"Yeah, I know Mandy hasn't been the most agreeable person lately. She has some issues with jealousy right now. They've always done everything together. Turning them into a threesome doesn't seem to be working out at all."

"That's all Sam's fault. From what I'm seeing, he doesn't want to share Gabby's time anymore. He wants her all to himself, either on the phone or on instant messaging. Can't blame him. That's what teenage boys are all about at this stage. And Sam's way behind in that department, so I'm sure he's not making any bones about taking Gabby away from Mandy whenever he can. I think a temporary move right now would benefit everyone. I sure as hell know it would me, I'm exhausted."

She smiled up at him and reached for his hand. "Okay, I'll go. I hate to see you wearing yourself out like this, especially since it's all my fault. When are they going to let me go home so I can pack a few things?"

"They're not. I'm arranging to have you flown from here directly to the hospital in Denver. After a few days there, if everything's all right, I'll take you home. Mandy has to stay here for another week. She can stay with Gabby and her parents. I'll fly back for her. Make a list of the things you want me to pack for you and I'll go get them before we fly to Denver."

"Got this all worked out, have you?"

"Certainly. Did you have any doubts?" he asked with a grin.

23 Weeks

VIGOROUS KICKS CAN BE SEEN AS WELL AS FELT.

A few days later, Michael arranged for Michele to be flown by a Med Star unit to Denver where she would remain in the hospital for at least two weeks or until he was sure she was out of danger. A week later, he flew back for Amanda who was not too happy about the move, temporary or not.

They wouldn't know for a month or more if the transfusion had helped but Michele continued to think that it had since there was no evidence to the contrary. They would start doing some blood tests the following week to see if there was any improvement.

Michael had Amanda transferred to Sam's high school to finish the second semester of her junior year, despite her woeful begging to stay in San Francisco with Gabby and her parents. There was so much going on now with both Michele and Amanda, that Michael felt he needed to keep them both under his wing.

25 Weeks

AIR SACS FORM IN THE LUNGS AND THE BABIES BEGIN PRIMITIVE
BREATHING.

A few days after leaving the hospital, Michele was settled into one of Michael's guest rooms. Michael's housekeeper, Anita, who usually came in twice a week was now with them all day seeing to the needs of both Michele and Amanda. Michele was sofa-bound most of the day, while Amanda, feeling better and better each day, grudgingly went to school with Sam.

Amanda had her own room on the other side of the house where Sam's room was and she was already trying to finagle a way to get Gabby to come visit. Sam, of course, was behind her all the way, and was helping her come up with ideas to bargain with. But by the time they approached Michele and then regrouped to address a pretty ragged Michael, they knew their chances were nil.

"I don't understand why she can't come out for a few days. She has teacher workdays coming up and her mom said it was okay," Mandy whined.

"Amanda, I don't think this is a good time to overtax yourself or your Mom," Michael said in his soft but commanding voice. "If your numbers keep improving and your mother feels up to it, Gabby can come next month. And that's the end of it," he said

directing a hard glare first at Amanda and then at his son. "Now
both of you, get your studies done."

He watched as they both turned and glumly climbed the
stairs to their rooms. Then he chuckled as he slid down to sit
on the end of the sofa where Michele was resting. He lifted
both of her feet and held them firmly in his lap, his hands
massaging and soothing her feet.

"So, how was your day?" he asked her as he gently stroked
her arch.

"Oh, fine. I've read every catalogue I could find, watched
two videos, crocheted a baby blanket, answered all my corre-
spondence, and started a new recipe file using some of Anita's
recipes. If I don't get out of this house soon, I'm going to
scream!"

He laughed as he continued stroking her feet. "A few more
days and maybe we can arrange a trip to the mall or a movie.
But you should know that you're going to have to rest one hour
for every three you're up, so plan your days wisely. I'm going to
be an ogre about this."

She smiled over at him and wished she was close enough to
stroke his cheek. Dear Michael. He was exhausting himself for
them. She should be the one rubbing *his* feet.

"Have I told you how much I appreciate you?"

His answering smile was a little crooked and had an ironic
cast to it.

"You doubt me?"

"No. I was just thinking about Steph, and how I took her
for granted. I should have appreciated her more. I should have
paid much more attention to her."

"What brought all this on?"

"I was changing my clothes and I realized how anxious I was to come down here to see you. I hadn't realized how empty this house was until you moved in. I look forward to talking to you. You make me laugh. You make me forget the hospital."

"Well, somebody sure needs to. You live and breathe that place."

"It's all I've had to care about for quite some time."

"What about Sam?"

"Sometimes I think that Sam takes better care of me than I do of him. I swear that kid was born more mature than I'll ever be."

She laughed and kicked at his hand. "You're mature. You're very mature," she said snidely, trying to make it sound like he was decrepit with age.

He ran his hand up and tickled the back of her knee, causing her to screech and giggle, and she tried to kick him away when he climbed further up beside her body.

"I'm not too old to drag you off this couch and . . . ."

"And what?" she prompted. But then his face was over hers and his eyes met hers and they both just stared, mesmerized by the moment.

Finally, Michael straightened and mumbled, "Tickle you 'til you beg for mercy." But they both knew that wasn't what he was going to say.

He sat up and covered her feet with the throw that had slid to the floor.

"Do you ever think you might remarry, Shell?" he asked, his tone serious.

"Yeah, I guess so, I've always thought that one day I might."

"You know that once the babies get here you're going to be out of commission at least until they start school. You're thirty-eight now, thirty-nine by the time the babies get here. Six years to that and you'll be forty-five, practically out to pasture. Then you've got to date until you hook up with the right guy. That could be another two or three years. You'll be close to fifty then. Are you sure you don't want to consider my offer? It's not likely you're going to improve all that much with age you know."

"Well, gee thanks!"

"You know what I mean. If you're going to be looking for a husband, you're the most marketable now."

"You make me sound like a side of beef aging by the minute!"

"Well, you might as well face it. If you want a man with any kind of prospects, what do you think he's going to be looking for?"

Well, he had her there. They both understood what he was trying to tell her.

"So, Michael. You're a man of good prospects, high caliber and all that, what are you looking for?"

"I wasn't. I was happy enough the way things were. But you've changed all that. I want more now. I want what I had before, or as close as I can get to it."

He was silent for a few moments while he just stared at her. And despite his words declaring open season, his eyes told her he wasn't looking beyond her. There was passion and desire in his eyes, and something else, too.

"In answer to your question . . . I want a woman who's intelligent, caring, fun to be with, spontaneous, and so sexy she makes me feel alive and more like a man than I ever have."

"Tall order."

"Not really. You fill it perfectly."

"I don't believe I heard pregnant with twins on that list."

"Oh, did I forget that? Well, let me add that right now," he whispered as his fingertip lifted her chin and his mouth descended to hers. His lips covered hers as his arms wrapped around her shoulders and he pulled her to him.

She trembled in his arms as his lips took full possession of hers. She fought him for the briefest of moments while her hands rose to protest, but the next second found them splayed on each side of his head, fingers threaded through his thick hair as she pulled him closer.

Michael reached up behind her and turned off the light on the table lamp behind her. And in the semidarkness, they necked like two teenagers getting ready to leave summer camp.

His tongue chased hers until it surrendered to him and then he moved on to her cheek, her chin, and her neck. He was nibbling and kissing and awakening long-dormant nerves and smooth, soft flesh. His hot breath was heating her and she felt rushing, warm sensations flowing all over her body. He was igniting sparking fires in her belly and lower. Much, much lower. Her nipples tingled and she could feel them swelling and engorging. Then suddenly, she felt them leaking.

She quickly pulled away and stared down at her chest and sure enough, there on her light cotton-shell sweater were two small, dark circles marking the area where her nipples had wet her cotton bra cups and then her sweater.

"Oh," she gasped, "I'm leaking something."

He looked down where her eyes were focused and chuckled. "So you are. Your nipples are excreting a lubricant. It's called colostrum. Congratulations, I believe this marks your entry into the third trimester. Here, let me have a look," he asked.

And she knew he wasn't asking because he was a doctor.

Embarrassed as she was, she couldn't deny the light of excitement in his eyes. She nodded and he pulled her sweater up. Then he reached behind her and unclasped her bra. Everything was pulled off at once and went quickly flying over her head. Then she was topless on his sofa in the middle of the family room with the long bridge to the loft and bedrooms just overhead.

"Uh . . . don't you think we should, uh . . . ."

"No. Don't move. And don't talk. This is a reverent moment. I need to pay homage to this incredible sight."

She looked down at her large and impossibly-full breasts that had nipples sticking farther out than she could ever remember them doing before. Then she shifted her attention to Michael's face and saw the complete look of utter contentment. He was enraptured with her body and it showed.

Gingerly, he reached out and, using his right hand, he hefted one of her breasts. Her left one. She would never be able to pinpoint who moaned first, but she thought it was him, by a fraction of a second. As his hand continued to fondle and then lightly squeeze her, her nipple oozed out a creamy substance. When his tongue licked the glistening drop, tracing it back to her nipple, she cried out and had to bite her lip. Then his sucking action undid her and she closed her eyes in ecstasy as she slid further into the cushions of the sofa. He had moved on to the other breast and was manipulating one breast with his hand while tonguing the other when the phone rang. The sharp ringing tone made Michele jump. The sound of a door opening on the upper level right above them made Michael jump. He quickly opened the sofa throw and threw it over her while shoving her sweater and bra beneath it.

"Dad, it's for you," Sam yelled over the banister to him.

"Okay, I'll take it down here," Michael managed to croak. And then they heard the door close again.

He reached for the phone on the end of the coffee table in front of them. "Dr. Moore," he breathed heavily. To the unsuspecting, he sounded winded, but Michele knew differently. He was aroused, panting from desire and quite a bit miffed to have been disturbed.

"Yes. Yes. Those were the orders I left. No, no I do not. Call me if there's any change, otherwise let's ride it out. Yes. Yes. Thank you for calling. It's always better to be sure." He replaced the phone in the cradle and fell back against the sofa cushions.

"The hospital calling about a patient?"

"Yes. There was a question about the medication I prescribed."

"Well, it's good you were home."

"Yes, yes it was. But they would have found me anywhere. They always do. It's part of the job. I thought I was used to it. Tonight I was not."

"Well, how long has it been since you were interrupted this way?" she asked with a broad smile on her face.

"Too long," he replied with a grin. "What's the chance of you coming to my room and me picking up where we left off?" His hand moved to snake under the throw but she thwarted it. He growled his displeasure, but stayed his hand.

Her hand went out to his cheek and she stroked it. "I'm not so sure that's a good idea. Aside from the fact that we have teenagers upstairs—one with wildly raging hormones—that we're supposed to be role models for."

"Let me tell you that right now I have some hormones that are not only raging but raging with enough power to burst right through the pores of my skin!"

Another door opened upstairs and Amanda came to stand over the rail. As she looked down at them some twenty feet below, she whined, "Mom, I think I need some help with this Calculus. Can you come help me?"

"Calculus? Can't you get Sam?"

"He's busy on the computer doing an English report."

"Okay, I'll be right there," Michele said with an obvious groan. "Can't remember any of that stuff, can you?" she asked as she held onto her clothes and the throw long enough to get into the hallway under the bridge.

Michael watched her disappear into the powder room, but watched her reflection off the glass of a picture hanging in the hallway since she hadn't bothered to close the bathroom door. *Man, the woman had an incredible set of tits!*

As the sweater settled down over her, he focused his mind on answering the question she'd asked. "No, I don't remember calculus. Hell, I hardly remember medical school. I'm just winging it."

She chuckled and walked back to stroke his now-stubbly chin. "Yeah, right." Then she was gone, slowly climbing the steps to the upstairs bedrooms.

AArrrggh! What was she doing to him? And why wouldn't she marry him so he could hold her some more, touch her, kiss her, lick her, without interruption.

Mandy didn't need as much help as Michele thought. If she didn't know her daughter better, she would have thought she just wanted to talk. She hadn't had a good day in school and she was a little melancholy because today was the anniversary of her father's death in that horrible plane crash. They both had decided independently not to mention it to the other as they sat at the breakfast table that morning, but with one look, they had known what was on each other's mind.

Michael had sensed their mood, but wasn't aware of what was going on until he noticed the date at the top of his newspaper. Then throughout the day, as they each went their separate ways, thoughts of Kevin were gradually pushed aside until he was finally forgotten in the business at hand.

But now, as Mandy prepared for bed, she needed her mom and the feel of comforting arms around her. They talked for forty minutes about all manner of things before acknowledging the elephant in the room. Then they had a good cry on each other's shoulders and Michele tucked Mandy in just like she used to do when she was a little girl.

"Daddy would be so proud of you," she whispered to her from the door.

"Thanks, Mom."

"Tomorrow will be better, sweetheart."

"It had better be. Today was the pits!"

Michele gave her a sympathetic smile and began closing the door behind her, leaving her daughter in the quiet enveloping darkness as the large beam of light coming from the hallway became a thin sliver. The door clicked closed, and the bleak, total darkness of a moonless night engulfed the room, leaving Mandy all alone with her thoughts.

Tomorrow they'd find out how her blood was doing, but she already knew. She didn't know how she knew, she just knew. Oh, sure, she felt better. She felt a lot better. But she didn't feel "fixed." No, she didn't feel that she had been "repaired." Maybe just temporarily mended.

But that was okay because she had already decided that dying would be the more noble way to go. Dying would tie up all the lose ends. Then everybody could live happily ever after. She hoped she would be remembered fondly, and as a critical defining point in the lives she had touched, especially Gabby's. Much like Vada and Thomas Jay were in the movie *My Girl*, when Thomas Jay died from those bee stings because he had to go looking for Vada's ring.

In a way things had worked out exactly as she'd planned. Her mom was on her way to finding a new husband. The fact that it was turning out to be her uncle was a hoot, but so what? And Gabby, she'd known all along that Gabby would need a new best friend. She just hadn't given the idea that much thought, figuring one would come along sooner or later. That he might be male and making signs with lifetime commitment written all over them, hadn't occurred, even in her incredibly-vivid imagination.

But dying wasn't so bad. She'd told that kid, Amy, who'd spent her last two weeks dying from a brain tumor in the bed next to her in the hospital, that she'd soon be there in Heaven to cheer her up. Just turns out that she was right. More right than she'd actually believed at the time. And somehow, despite all her mom's best efforts and wishes, she just knew this had been what had been ordained for her from the very beginning. It didn't scare her. Well, not much. This was her future, her destiny, and she might as well embrace it. All things led to another and this was just one thing leading to the next for her.

She was glad she felt better. At least she'd enjoy the rest of her life while it lasted. But honestly, you knew what you knew, and in her heart of hearts, the train ride was just about over. It was time to prepare to come into the station.

Her mind flew a couple of months ahead and she imagined the birth announcements with pictures of the babies in the cutouts, her brother, her sister. Her legacy somehow, for if it hadn't been for her, they wouldn't even be. The babies, born in desperation, would now become the nucleus for her mom's new family and she couldn't be happier. After all, she'd at least have her dad.

Michele waved goodnight to Michael from the loft, ignoring his enthusiastic hand waving for her to come back down. Mandy had set the tone for the rest of her evening and she thought it best that she retire to her room.

After changing into her nightgown, she sat up in bed trying to read about the next series of changes to expect with the babies. She was almost six months pregnant now, and although Dr. Brarely kept assuring her that things were progressing normally, she felt that the babies must not be growing as much as they should. She looked like a woman with a slight beer gut, not a woman who would be delivering twins in the very near future. At twenty-five weeks her babies would be close to ten inches long, half the length they would be if they went full term. According to Michael, twenty-six weeks was the critical hurdle to get over. If the babies stayed in utero after that it was a bonus. Gravy time, he said. Time for them to "get fat."

She smiled as she remembered when he'd said that. He'd playfully slapped her on the rump and said, "Just like you. You're fattening up quite nicely, if I do say so myself."

"I prefer to call it blossoming," she'd replied.

He'd kissed her on the cheek and intimately whispered into her ear, "I think heavy breasts with dark aureolas and swollen ankles are incredibly sexy," just as he'd grabbed his bag from the counter and left to go to work. Mandy and Sam had just arrived in the kitchen to say good-bye and had witnessed the heated blush creeping up her neck and going all the way to her hairline.

Mandy had just looked at her like she was some kind of traitor and Sam had impishly smiled. Both had grabbed their books and lunches and left without saying a word.

Now, as she sat up against a pile of pillows propped up by the headboard, reading about electric breast pumps and how to establish your milk supply, she sighed. She let the book drop to her side and closed her eyes. Just why did Michael want to marry her? Why was he so persistent in this latest quest of his?

Hell, why did any man want to marry these days, she asked herself. It's not like they really needed to anymore; carnal satisfaction didn't require marriage these days. What could be Michael's reasons for wanting to marry her?

He certainly didn't need anyone to vacuum his floors or wash his clothes. In fact, if she married him, it was pretty much a given that she'd never have to push or pull a vacuum again in her life. Boy, the thought of never having the tedious and strenuous job of dragging a vacuum up each riser to vacuum the carpeted stairs made marriage look quite inviting. She smiled to herself as she thought of all the chores she'd never have to do if she married Michael. After all, he had a housekeeper *and* a gardener.

She'd certainly never have a day stolen from her again because something went wrong with the house. Oh, to never have to lose a day, or a big part of it, to the inane things that were always going wrong: a hot-water heater bursting when no one was home; an upright freezer filled with rancid meat because someone left the door open on the hottest day of the year; or a sudden invasion of black ants in the pantry because they followed a lemonade trail from the back porch to the food mother lode. God, she would never forget the hours lost forever to carpet cleaning and window washing. Necessary, but days . . . whole complete days that she'd never, ever get back.

Michael had staff to handle anything like that when it came along. And now, with three "it wasn't me" kids instead of just one, imagine all the new and interesting things that were going to "go wrong" around the house.

Kevin had occasionally done some yard work but he had never helped with the housework. When he came home to bright, clean carpets, he never took note. Streakless, grime-free windows never got a comment. She always thanked him for the time *he* spent mowing, raking, or painting, and even told him how much she appreciated how hard *he* worked at his job, even if it did take him away from them all too often. But he never thanked her for being his devoted wife, his tireless house-keeper, or for being the best mother she could be to Mandy. It was just accepted that she would be. And she was. And in her spare time, she had helped to run an art gallery and even managed to sell a few pieces of art every now and then. But since she loved art, Kevin hadn't really considered that work. Was she ready to get into that game again? Did she even want to?

And what exactly did Michael want from her? Why did he want this marriage so badly? Did he want her to cook? She *was* a good cook. Until she and Mandy had shown up to live here, the pizza delivery service had been number one on the speed dial.

Nah, if Michael wanted better food, even gourmet meals, he could afford to hire someone to come in and cook them for him. Did he want sex? Hell, he could have a line outside his door if that's all he wanted. A man like Michael could command a whole brigade of women eager to do his erotic, libidinal bidding. No, that couldn't be it either.

It must be the babies he wants. He'd mentioned once that Stephanie had the deciding vote on whether they'd have more children, but time had taken the decision and opportunity from her.

He must have wanted more children. Now, he wanted hers. Well, his. Actually . . . both of theirs, she finally conceded.

Well, that must be it. Unless she was mistaken, he certainly had the role of father down pat.

She felt something kick against her side and she reached down to rub the spot where one baby's foot had just nudged her. She smiled and reached over to turn out the light. There were definitely some advantages to staying single and enjoying her freedom, but at times like this, it sure would be nice to roll over and have a strong arm pull her in close.

But is that all she wanted? Security? Didn't she want passion? She wished she knew if the tingling feelings she had whenever Michael was around were because of him or because of her memories of Kevin and the fire that they had once had together.

Was she reliving old feelings or creating new ones? And how would she ever know?

26 Weeks

THE BABIES' SKIN IS THICKENING. TASTE BUDS APPEAR.

During her third week at Michael's house, Michele woke feeling as if she was being watched. She blinked her eyes open, rolled over onto her side, and met Michael's piercing blue-gray eyes as he stood at her door.

"You were moaning," he said huskily.

He stood there wearing a pair of drawstring pajama bottoms with no shirt. She felt her entire body kick into high gear when she saw his muscular chest with its thick scattering of curling, black hairs. They formed a vee and connected to a dark line bisecting his stomach and disappearing under the waistband riding low on his narrow hips. He looked just like Kevin had. All male, all muscled and warm flesh that was toned and tanned by his active lifestyle.

She hadn't felt this type of heat coursing through her since the night almost a year ago when she'd suddenly awakened in one of the hospitals where Amanda was being treated. She had been dozing, reclining on a cot set up beside Amanda's bed.

It was late, very late, but still closer to midnight than to morning when she'd felt someone come into the room. She had opened her eyes to see a young doctor silhouetted in the open area between the two screens. His dark eyes took in everything about her and it was obvious that he liked what he saw.

"I thought I heard something. Are you all right?" he'd asked.

She'd looked down at the way the blanket had ridden up, exposing her naked thigh. She sometimes had to sleep in just her slip on those nights when she unexpectedly ended up overnight in the hospital. On this night, there was nothing covering her shoulders or chest, except the lacy, scalloped-edged bra of her slip, since she had apparently thrown off the sheet. She knew she must have looked seductive in the coyly kittenish pose, but she hadn't bothered to cover up.

"Yes, I'm all right," she'd answered. And then looked down at her thigh again.

And she knew right then that she'd wanted him. She didn't know his name, she didn't know a thing about him. Only that he looked good and so apparently, did she. She'd felt the desire in his eyes and knew that he'd wanted her, too.

It would have been so easy to succumb to her desires. To take what she desperately wanted. What she desperately needed. How wonderful it would be to be held in a strong man's arms again. How easy it would have been to let someone she'd never know, someone she'd never have to see again, take her and possess her and make her feel like a woman again, instead of the neurotic and frantic mother that she had managed to become. She had looked at him long and hard, knowing that all she had to do was to twitch the blanket an inch higher and he would have been there for her—hot, passionate and devilishly handsome in his white staff coat. He, of course, would have been vigorous and vigilante and most importantly, anonymous forever.

But Amanda had stirred, and the moment had been taken from them.

Now, as she stared at Michael in the dimly-lit hallway, the fantasy replayed itself in her mind. Only this time, the man with the question in his eyes was Michael. A man she could allow herself to lay with, pretending he was Kevin, or a man she could lay with knowing full well that he was Michael. Michael, who was so much like Kevin, but at the same time, not anything like him at all.

She moved aside and held the covers up as her invitation for him to join her. He didn't hesitate. He crossed the threshold, closed the door quietly behind him, and pulled once on the drawstring of his pajama bottoms. Just before he slid into the bed beside her, she saw his stiff manhood jutting out from the thick copse of dark hair between his legs. The sight of it aroused her incredibly. It was a familiar sight, but one she hadn't seen for many years. In this area, Michael and Kevin were identically and wondrously endowed. She had to force herself to remember that the man crawling in beside her was Michael and not Kevin, her husband. It was eerie, almost like welcoming a ghost into her bed. Or was it more like cheating and having an affair? Whichever one it was, it didn't matter; she decided she was just going to let it happen.

If she hadn't known what her invitation had said to him, she certainly had no doubts now. The hands that reached for her felt powerful and comforting as he pulled her across the sheets and into his massive chest.

His lips searched her skin in the darkness until they found hers and he took them greedily, his groan attesting to his impatience as he shifted each soft part of her into the corresponding hard part of him. Her hips were gently cushioned into his as his legs moved against hers. The babies were positioned high and he was careful to settle his hips below her expanding girth.

"Mmmm. Shelley, mmm. Oh God, here. Touch me here," he demanded as he took her hand and led it to his engorged manhood. "Oh shit. I can't do this. It's been too long. Damn! That feels wonderful. Ohhh," he said as his hand skimmed her from her hip to her waist and then past her ribs.

Quickly, he dragged her nightgown up the length of her body and jerked it off. Before it was flying over her head, his hand had returned to her ribcage where he found a firm, plump breast aching for his touch. As he allowed it to fill his hand she arched into his palm.

"Ohmygod," she breathed. And then when he stroked her nipple with his thumb, she gasped and threw her head back. His head ducked down and he took possession of the tip with his lips and the sounds she began making became the sweetest, sexiest sounds he'd ever heard in his life.

"I don't think I can take my time with you," he breathed as he licked the valley between her cleavage.

"I don't think I could stand it if you did." Her fingers delved into his chest hairs and the second her thumb found a nipple, she unmercifully toyed with it.

He jammed his hand between her thighs and spread them while his fingers found her silky, pliant flesh. He explored it with his strong, deft fingers before plunging their length deeply into her. She bucked wildly against his hand, feeling his intrusion with each stroke of her hips as she moved against his fevered hand. She felt his erection trying to find home in the curve of her belly before moving to the sweet niche at the top of her thigh.

"Got to," he murmured. "Got to have you. Take you. Now. Nnggh," he grunted as he turned his body into hers and positioned himself to penetrate her.

She assisted by grabbing his thick shaft and placing the slippery head at her opening. And with just one thrust of his hips he shoved himself deeply inside her.

"Sweet Jesus!" he yelled against the side of her neck. "Damn, you feel incredible!"

"So long," she murmured. "It's been so long," she repeated as she felt him fill her to capacity. What a wonderful feeling, she thought dreamily, as her muscles contracted to welcome him.

Her hands stroked his shoulders and his back. She could feel the warm ridges of his muscles while he flexed them as he leveraged himself over her.

He was careful not to put any weight on her. And he had to keep reminding himself not to pinch her hard, engorged nipples, much as he wanted to. Later, he could use that invisible connection to draw her to new heights. Now, he had to remember the babies and avoid any possibility of sending her into premature labor.

He teased her with several long strokes while his lips sought hers. Then his tongue delved into her mouth and his teeth gently pulled at her bottom lip, and all the while, his frenzied hips circled and thrust and parried against hers as he kept his upper body away from her.

When the tempo got away from him and she could tell he was close to coming, her hands slid down his backside to grip his buttocks. Digging her fingers into his fleshy backside, she lifted her hips and arched up against him. Through some signal only lovers know, he managed to stop his deep thrusts just in time to be there for her, to hold tightly against her at the critical moment that she needed him.

He felt her arching and straining upward until she finally forced the ridge of his hard flesh to touch her hooded, pulsing nub. When it finally made that magical contact that she needed oh-so-much, her body convulsed and long-dormant floodgates opened everywhere. The tiny, erratic pulsing of her aftershocks, connected with his own driving, throbbing urgency shattered him, and together they eclipsed each other. She experienced one incredible climax that built and hit its crescendo, and then another followed as her body responded to the perfect strumming of his. Then they were both jolted out of the universe and sent adrift into a deep, dark, bottomless chasm.

The sounds Michael made into the pillow beside her head were primal, and so overwhelmingly base that they shocked her. She should have known that a man who worked and played as hard as he did would make love with abandon. These were the sounds of a man coming from a passion so sublime that it sounded like he was dying. It gave Michele incredible pleasure to hear it and to know that she was the cause of it. For a few minutes she had thought that he held all the power between them. Now her thinking changed. She had power over him and it was absolute. It thrilled her to know it and she reveled in it.

"I can't believe I just fucked you," he whispered into the side of her neck. He smiled broadly at his own crude words and pressed his lips against her as he continued to kiss the long column of her throat.

"Yeah, and I can't believe I wasted all that money on artificial insemination when we could have conceived naturally."

"Hey, I offered," he whispered, still dragging kisses from her neck down to her shoulder.

"That was wild."

"Yes, that was most definitely wild. I am in awe of you and your absolutely incredible body." His hand moved to cup a nicely-rounded buttock before he flattened his palm and rubbed it over her extended abdomen.

"Are you feeling okay? How are the babies doing?"

"They must be asleep, I don't feel anything right now. I just feel absolutely wonderful," she said with a devilish smile as she stretched her full length under him. "Remarkably and totally wonderful."

"Yes. Yes, you do," he whispered as his hands continued to rove over her. Lying down, and stretching out as she was, he could barely feel the gentle rounding of her pregnancy. Lower, he could feel the small scar of her recent surgery, though it was partially hidden in her short, new pubic hairs.

"Were we quiet? It didn't sound like we were to me," she asked.

"No, it didn't to me either. Thank God, we're on the opposite side of the house. This would be a little hard to explain."

"No kidding."

He leaned up on his elbows and looked down into her face. "You know this changes things. We can't go back to the way we were. I'm going to want to do this often. Very often," he murmured as his fingertips caressed her cheek and he drew one down the tip of her nose.

"Mmm. Me, too."

"You're safe for ten, maybe, eleven weeks."

"Apparently not from you," she said with a wide grin. "You've got it all planned out, don't you?"

"Marry me, Shelley."

Her eyes blinked at his words and she felt a tightness settle in her chest.

"Oh, Michael," she whispered on the end of a sob as she buried her face in his chest.

"What's the matter?"

"I can't marry you Michael. It wouldn't be fair."

"Why wouldn't it?"

"I'm not really sure that you're Michael to me."

It took a moment for him to get her meaning. Then the disappointment she saw in his eyes disappeared as quickly as it came. "What does it matter? It's still me here with you, whether you think it's me or him. I don't care. I know you loved him, and so did I. If this is how I can be with you, it doesn't matter to me who you think I am. I'll deal with it."

"It matters to me."

He lifted her head where it was snuggled against his chest. With his fingers under her chin, he lifted her mouth for his kiss. "I love you Shelley. I love *you;* I love the babies, and I want to be there for you. And I want you to be here for me. In my bed, especially," he said with a grin. "There isn't any way in hell that I can give you up now. Not after this," he said with his hand indicating their entwined length on the tousled bed. "No way in hell." He captured her mouth with his again and began using his tongue to convince her that everything he was saying was true. She felt him grow hard again as the heat rose from her toes to her thighs.

"Well, maybe just one more time . . . ."

"The hell you say. You just wait. I *will* make you mine."

27 Weeks

THE EYELIDS AND NOSTRILS HAVE OPENED. THE BABIES CAN PERCEIVE
LIGHT, SMELL, AND TASTE.

Michael came home from work the next morning after rearranging his appointments because he felt that he and Michele could use a little time alone. As far as he was concerned, they were having a romance and he wanted to settle into it very carefully. So an hour after Sam and Mandy had left for school he returned home.

Michele was both surprised and pleased to see him.

"What are you doing back home? I thought you had a full day?"

"I did. My secretary and I cleared the calendar for the day. I wanted to spend some time with you. It's a beautiful day, what do you say to a walk in Estes Park?"

"Ooh. That sounds nice. I've never been there."

"Well grab your coat and a nice warm scarf and let's go. You have eaten already, haven't you?"

"Yes," she said with a sigh. "Why are you always checking on me?"

"Because I care. And because . . . I don't know. That's just what men do." He gave her a quirky smile and motioned with his hand for her to get a move on.

Michele smiled back at him and ran up the stairs to go to the bathroom and to get her purse. In the bathroom she stood looking at her profile, holding her protruding belly with her hands.

She'd had such a good time with Michael last night. It gave her little shivers just thinking about it. About the things they had done and how she'd felt when he had touched her so intimately. Making love with the brother of her dead husband was so weird, especially since they had been so much alike physically. It was almost like having Kevin back in her life. Would it be so bad loving Kevin through him? And was it even Kevin she was thinking about? Oh Lord, how would she know? Grabbing her purse, she went downstairs to find Michael.

When they were walking in the park, he wrapped her hand over his arm and snuggled her body close to his. The day was bright and sunny, but in the shaded areas, it was still pretty cold.

"You're awfully quiet. Are you okay?" he asked.

"Yeah, just thinking."

"About what?"

"Just lots of things," she said. And he knew she was avoiding his question. He decided he needed to be more direct. He knew that they had to communicate or they'd have no shot at making this relationship take off and he didn't want what they had to be just about sex.

"Did last night affect you in a bad way?"

"Oh no, no. Last night was wonderful."

"Completely? No reservations?"

She hesitated for a full minute and then she said, "Well, I can't help thinking you're Kevin sometimes."

His eyes blinked wide. "Why would you think that? Is my love making reminiscent of Kevin's?"

"Oh no. Not at all. For identical twins, you have nothing in common there. Other than your physical attributes of course," she said with a sideways smile.

"Well, now I'm really curious. Was he any good? Am I any good?"

"You both were terrific in your own special way," she hedged. "Kevin was soft and gentle and not very demanding. It was always a quiet and reverent time for us. You, you have more energy or you certainly put more energy into it. You're forceful and more of a take charge kind of guy. You know what you want and you take it. And last night you took it completely."

"You make me sound like I'm Attila the Hun. Was I brutal? Forceful? Did I hurt you?"

"No, nothing like that. You're just more of a man's man, whereas Kevin was more of a lady's man, if you know what I mean."

"Now you're making Kevin sound gay."

"No! He was placating. He had women throwing themselves at him all the time at work, so I think he established in his own mind that he wanted his wife to be more staid. Proper like."

"You mean a prude."

"Not a prude really, just not all that affected. Certainly not to the point where I would throw myself at him as soon as he came through the door."

"Well, that's a damn shame."

She threw him a cautious smile. "Well, I certainly had no idea what we were missing."

"You and I, we're still missing out on a few things."

"Oh, I don't think so," she said as she blushed full red. She was pretty sure she knew what he was referring to.

"Take my word for it," he reiterated with a wink.

"I have this thing about being clean," she said timidly. "Along with being very self-conscious."

"I'm a doctor, I have this thing about everything being clean, too. It won't be a problem. And you have nothing to be self-conscious about, you're a very beautiful and desirous woman."

He held her close, wrapped tightly in his arms and then he straightened his arms and set her apart from him, just far enough so he could kiss her. So softly that she had a hard time believing that this was the same man who had practically ravished her just last night.

The kiss deepened as his tongue rimmed her lips and then breached them. Very tentatively he let his tongue mingle with hers while he savored the taste of her. Large snowflakes started falling all around them and when he broke the kiss, they were both startled to see the white flakes in each other's hair. The kiss had been long and leisurely . . . full of feelings and unspoken promises; promises to try to forget the past and hold on to the future; promises neither had to attest to regarding fidelity. While it lasted, they belonged to each other. He had tried to brand it into her with his lips that he knew this relationship was for real, even if she didn't yet. Children or no children, he wanted her. Desperately.

"Come on, I'd better take you home, you're getting chilled."

"I'm not at all cold."

"You are very cold. I'm a doctor, I know all about temperatures. You need to go home, get naked under covers and seek the body warmth of a naked man."

"Really?" she said with a half smile.

"Really. It's the only way we're going to get your temperature back up."

"Then we'd better hurry."

He wasted no time getting her back to the park entrance and tucked into his car. Unfortunately, on the way home, they came across an accident, and Michael was compelled to help out. Three people were hurt, one badly, a four-year-old boy. After stabilizing the young victim, he instructed her to go home in his car while he accompanied the ambulance to the hospital.

Later, he called her to tell her the four year old was going to be okay, and also how sorry he was that he hadn't been able to restore her temperature. She laughed and told him she took a warm bath instead. He was miffed at her success without him, but took it good-naturedly.

"Another time, maybe."

"Another time, definitely," she replied and they both smiled as they disconnected.

28 Weeks

THE BABIES ARE BECOMING MORE ACTIVE. THEY ARE ABOUT FOURTEEN
INCHES LONG.

Amanda's tests showed a marked improvement and she was feeling worlds better. So much better, in fact, that she was spending all her free time badgering her mother to let Gabby come for an extended winter break. Since Sam and Mandy's winter break was the week before Gabby's, the three were trying to put together two weeks where they could all be together. Michele finally relented after Denise called and convinced her it would be all right for Sam and Mandy to stay with them. At Denise's urging, she and Michael finally allowed Sam and Mandy to fly to San Francisco to visit Gabby the first week, then they would all fly back together and Gabby would visit with them for the second week, even though Sam and Mandy would be back in school.

Mandy seemed so much better, it was hard for Michele not to want to see her happy and spending time with her best friend. She knew Denise would take good care of her, and if there were any problems, Gabby certainly knew what to do for Mandy. She offered Denise the use of her house, but Denise assured them that they had plenty of room since Gabby's brother would be away on a ski trip with his church. It sounded like everything was working out just perfectly.

She did wonder if Denise knew what she was up against with Sam and Gabby, though. To insure that things went well, Michele asked Michael to talk with Sam about behaving, being a responsible adult, and also about being sensitive to Mandy's feelings and being sure to include her in their activities. Sam agreed that they would, and the next few days were busy as they arranged flights and packed for the trip.

The night before they were to take Sam and Mandy to the airport, Michael took Michele out to dinner. As they sat over a delicious prime-rib dinner, Michael took Michele's hand in his and kissed it.

"It's been interesting this past week. Every time I tried to get you alone, one kid or the other managed to show up and spirit you away from me." He continued to kiss her knuckles as his eyes met hers across the table.

"Well, Sam and I have been getting pretty close lately. Even though he's almost an adult, I think he could use a little mothering every now and then."

"I'm not opposed to that at all. I think it's great that you two are getting along so well. But you have to admit, it has been quite difficult getting a private audience with you."

She blushed nervously as his thumb stroked her palm and his eyes looked seductively into hers.

"Well, Amanda followed me around like a puppy dog until I agreed to this trip and then I had to help her with her packing. I suppose in retrospect, if I'd said yes sooner, this would have all been over with days ago."

"Well, I, for one, wish that you had."

"Why?"

"I've missed being in your bed. I've been lonely and hungry. Very, very hungry." The little nibbles he was accentuating his words with were making shivers go up her spine, shivers so visible that he chuckled.

"We can't," she whispered.

"As soon as the kids leave tomorrow, I'm going to have Anita move your things into my room. At least for the week the kids are gone, you're going to sleep with me in my bed all night long." The look on his face told her that it would be useless to argue. His mind was made up and he wasn't about to take no for an answer. Not that she wanted to tell him no. Her body was awakening to his touch and she was a bit sorry she wouldn't be in his bed this very night.

"What will Anita think?"

"I really don't care what she thinks. I want you in my bed, all night, every night. And you might as well get used to the idea." The waiter came to clear their dishes and Michael was forced to drop her hand, but his eyes still held hers, forcing her to accept his last statement as fact.

The following day was a hectic one. Michele managed to get Sam and Mandy and all their luggage on the plane bound for San Francisco before going for her biweekly checkup. Then she arranged with Anita for the grocery shopping to be done so she and Michael wouldn't have to worry about doing any errands during their time alone. Anita had graciously been given the week off with full pay. For all appearances, Michael had thought of everything in his quest to set up playing house with Michele.

Since Michael's definitive statement regarding their sleeping arrangements for the next week, Michele had found herself almost giddy with excitement. Somehow she found time to shop, get her hair cut, her nails done, and have a facial. All worthy tasks to take on in a city completely unfamiliar to her.

Michael had his own frenetic day. He'd had two elective surgeries sandwiched in between two emergency surgeries. When he finally arrived home at nine o'clock to a darkened house, he wasn't in the best of moods.

But when he discovered that the reason the lights were all out on the first floor was because Michele had arranged a candlelight dinner in the sitting room of the master bedroom, his ire and his fatigue immediately left him.

She was sitting in an armchair in a little alcove reading when he walked in. There were candles on every flat surface illuminating the room with soft yellow light. On a low table, there was a wine carafe with one wine glass and a water goblet filled with Perrier from the bottle sitting beside it. The sight of her sitting there in a gossamer gown greeting him created a feeling of belonging that he hadn't felt in many years, in this, his own home.

He walked into the room, bent to place his briefcase by the dresser, and upon straightening, noticed that the light from the reading lamp above her both shadowed and revealed the bountiful shape and valley of her breasts. After letting his eyes take their liberty, they drifted to her face and to the welcome he saw there. His heart quickened with the knowledge that she had been waiting for him and was happy that he was now home.

As he walked over to where she sat, he threw off his sport coat and tossed it onto the bed. Then he pulled at his tie. He stood towering over her and she turned her face up for him to kiss. "Rough day?"

He bent and took her lips with his and murmured his agreement against her softness. Then his tongue swept her bottom lip and he placed kisses from the corner of her lip all the way to the whorl of her ear. "Let me take a quick shower, and then I'll take care of my last examination of the day," he whispered.

Goose bumps broke out along her arms and frissons of heat targeted her nerve endings. She reached her hand up to stroke his stubble-roughened cheek. "And shave?"

He smiled down at her, "Of course."

He disappeared into the master bath and she settled back to reading her book, time wasted for sure because she couldn't concentrate on anything except the lingering effects of his touch. She was sure her body had never responded this strongly or this sensually before. She had heard that pregnancy hormones could heighten feelings of sexual arousal, that they could even cause an increased libido in some women. With Amanda, all she remembered about her pregnancy was fear and discomfort. Did having a doctor in the house make her more relaxed? Or was this particular doctor in the house the reason for her increased desire and wanton feelings? She looked down at the sexy nightgown she had selected today strictly for its ease of removal, and toyed with the satin ribbons crisscrossing her breasts.

Was she a woman with needs who had just found a man who could appease them? Or was she a woman needing a man? She closed her eyes and rested her head back on the chair and tried to recall the last time she and Kevin had made love. She squeezed her eyes tight and tried to envision him poised over her, plunging himself into her. She tried to remember his eyes and what they had been telling her as he had repeatedly drove into her, seeking first her and then his release. But she couldn't keep Kevin's face in front of hers. It kept fading in and out. The subtly different nuances of Michael's face kept coming into play. And then suddenly, it was as if a mist had cleared and Michael's face appeared. "Michael," she whispered softly.

"Right here, babe," he said as he stood behind her chair, dressed in a short-sleeved shirt tucked into trousers with no belt, no shoes, no socks. His hands caressed her shoulders while his lips sought out the side of her neck. "Mmmm, you smell wonderful, like a garden of tea roses." He nibbled the slope of her neck and burrowed his nose into her hair.

She smiled at his touch and the gods of fortune that had allowed her to call out his name instead of Kevin's just then. What had happened there? she mused. Then his own spicy fragrance wafted over her and she inhaled the strong after-shave that hadn't yet dried on his skin.

"I called your office to see if you'd eaten. The nurse who answered was kind enough to tell me you'd ordered in subs earlier, so I just fixed a plate of cheese, crackers, and some fruit." She motioned to a side table by the window with her closed book.

With one hand, Michael helped himself to a piece of fruit and with the other he slid the book from her hand and turned it over. "What are you reading?" Then he answered his own question by reading the title, *What Now? I'm Pregnant*. Why are you reading this? You've already read a dozen books on the subject. What don't you know by now?"

"Oh, just reading . . . ." she said evasively.

He pulled out the ottoman and sat facing her. "Seriously, is something bothering you?"

When she didn't reply, he took both of her hands in his and lightly caressed them. "C'mon. You can tell me. What is it?"

After a few moments of hesitation, her eyes met his.

"Well?" he insisted.

"Sex. Sex is bothering me."

"Sex is bothering you?" His voice carried both alarm and dismay.

"No, no. *Sex* isn't bothering me. The idea that I want to have it is bothering me."

"Oh," he said relieved. Then after a moment's thought he asked, "Didn't you want to have sex before?"

"You mean with your brother?"

"Was there somebody else?" he asked mildly shocked.

"Oh, no! No. I just meant . . . I don't know what I meant. I just never felt this way."

"What way?" he asked gently.

She thought for a minute and then figured she might as well get it all out. "Wantonly, like I want sex, not just the man. No, that didn't sound right."

"Why don't you start from the beginning and tell me what this is all about," he said while he grabbed a slice of fruit for her and one for himself.

"I'm having a baby. Two of them. I shouldn't want to have sex!"

He laughed out loud and lifted her hands to his mouth to be kissed. "Yes, yes, you should. It's perfectly natural for a pregnant woman to want to make love, and the new school of thought is, that as long as things are normal and the woman is healthy, she can continue doing it up until she delivers." His eyebrows did a Groucho Marx thing and she smiled.

"I never did before."

"Well, each pregnancy is different. Plus you're older. A woman has a greater appreciation for sex as she gets older. Plus . . . you have a new man in your life. A very sexy and sensuous new man who turns you on incredibly."

She reached over to the side table, grabbed a slice of pear, and playfully shoved it into his mouth.

"You want me," he managed to say as he chewed the piece of fruit. "That's a good thing, 'cause I want you. Badly. Very, very badly. Stand up so I can see that nightgown. It looks deceptively easy to divest. Or am I mistaken there?"

She smiled as he pulled her to her feet. "You gotta know what strings to pull."

"Hell, why take a chance? I'll just pull them all," he said huskily as he pulled her into his arms.

Just then she felt a kick and her hand went to her abdomen. His hand joined hers and together they felt one of their babies making itself known.

"It never ceases to amaze me," he said in complete awe. After the baby settled down, Michael turned and then sat in the chair, taking her down with him. Michele sat in his lap while Michael pulled first one ribbon and then another trying to undo her gown.

Smiling seductively, Michele moved his hand aside, grabbed a ribbon at the top shoulder and pulled the bow out. As soon as the loops for the bow unfurled, the sleeves to the gown dropped and so did the whole bodice, leaving her bare from the waist up. The string that had held the whole gown together had been threaded through the straps, not in the lace work bodice as it had appeared.

Michael's dazed, dark gaze followed the material as it bunched at her waist and then his eyes returned to feast on her swollen breasts with their large, darkened aureolas. Reverently, and then possessively, he took her heavy breasts into his hands. His long surgeon's fingers expertly caressed and teased the tips. Her nipples were long and hard already, but he made them throb and ache with his taunting, tweaking, and gentle tugs.

"Have I told you how very much I love your breasts? How incredibly earthly and womanly they are? You are like a fertile goddess ready to be suckled by a warrior god."

"Is that you?"

"You bet!" he said as his lips closed over one large crest.

"I thought these were for the babies."

With her nipple still in his mouth, he looked up at her. "I've changed my mind, they can have the bottle."

As he licked and suckled her nipples, Michele groaned. A low heat had started to burn in her belly and she felt trickles of desire running helter-skelter throughout her body. Heat pooled in her where warm liquid flowed to welcome his touch, and she arched up, inadvertently wiggling her bottom against his thighs and his heavy, engorged and fully-aroused manhood.

He felt stirrings so strong he couldn't contain them as his member leapt to embed itself between the crease of her buttocks. Against his will, he found himself gently lifting her over again, rubbing her along the length of it. It was crude, he knew, but he ached to fill her, to enter her, to drive himself so deeply into her that she no longer thought this was just sex. He wanted her to feel like he was a part of her, the deepest, most secret

and cherished part of her. He wanted to be her completion; the
entity that made her whole.

When he could no longer stand the torture, his hand went
to the hem of her gown and he felt the smooth expanse of her
calf, her knee, and her muscled thigh. The wispy gown was
carried up her legs on the back of his hand as he searched out
her hip, baring her smooth, silky leg to his gaze as it continued
higher. His flat palm smoothed over her hip and grazed her
stomach before hesitating and delving between her thighs. He
parted her thighs with his hand and cupped her curls. Then
one long finger dipped down and stroked her until she blos-
somed open for him. The hot slickness that was her welcomed
him and he reveled in the knowledge that desire, desire she had
for him, was causing these marvelous changes in her body.

Her low moans as well as her hands fumbling and finally
managing to open his shirt, sent leaping tongues of fire through
his veins. He wanted her, wanted to be inside her, wanted to
feel her sheathed and hot around him. But he couldn't rush
her, wouldn't let her think that he needed her so badly in the
physical sense that he would just ravish her and leave her
wanting. But he promised himself that as soon as he felt her
shudder under his fingers, he was going to carry her to his bed,
spread her thighs wide, and enter her with all the finesse of a
Viking fresh into port.

His practiced fingers stroked and massaged her and then
he gingerly slid his longest finger up into her. Her sudden gasp
and maneuvering wiggle caused him to smile. As she arched
against his finger he used his thumb to caress her small, but
growing nubbin. Rhythmically, he rubbed it in tiny circles, then
he flicked it back and forth, constantly dipping down and
rewetting his fingertip with her labial juices to allow for only

the silky, soft friction of his finger pad to glide over and over her. His sensitive fingertips felt her bud swell and he knew she was only moments from experiencing her orgasm.

But despite his body's primal urgings to speed things up so as to allow for his own turn, he drew his finger back. He had been watching her beautiful face contort into a grimace of longing and passion, now he saw confusion reign supreme as he heartlessly left her wanting. The disappointment in her eyes caused by him taking her this far and stopping nearly crushed him, but he had other plans. He would give her more, more than just a fingering job. She said she wanted sex. She must be desiring something intense, something more than what she could easily give herself.

He put one arm under her knees and the other around her shoulders, then he lifted her and carried her over to his bed, placing her on the very end of it. Once he had her situated with a pillow beneath her head, he stood at her feet and parted her thighs wide, bent her knees up, and knelt between them at the foot of the bed. Even though his eyes were feasting, he couldn't wait to taste her. His head bent quickly and his soft lips claimed her.

Her bud had disappeared behind its hood, but it took no time at all to coax it out and warm it with his tongue, and then with his lips. As she screamed his name and arched up to him, he lavished her with kisses and tongued her unmercifully. Then laying absolute claim to the most erotic and sensuous part of a woman's body, he lifted her throbbing clit with his rolled tongue and sucked it between his lips. Suddenly her knees spread wider allowing him greater access, and then her frantic hands reached down and clasped his head tightly to her. As her fingers delved deeply into his thick curls, she pulled him close and screamed his name. Then she held him as she shattered and released herself against his lips.

He stayed as he was, not even breathing as he felt her pulsing against his lips and tongue. The sensation rippled through him and he didn't know when he had ever been happier in his whole life. This woman was his, every damn part of her.

When she could no longer hold her legs up and the aftershocks had become warm shivers of satisfaction, he released her. As he moved away from her he pulled her legs down, but did not close them. He stood and removed his pants and then braced himself between her thighs at the end of the bed. His erection had been in several different stages of arousal within the last few minutes, but since her orgasm, it had been rampant, ready and almost purple with suppression. He thumbed it down into position and unhesitatingly slid it home, and she eagerly welcomed it.

Snugged all the way up inside her, he just stood for a moment enjoying the sensation of being inside her, being one with her. He was as close as he could be to her, and to his babies. And this was bliss such as he'd never known before. He looked at where they were joined, her coppery curls meshed with his thick bush of black ones, and it was all he could do to contain himself. He could easily lose it just standing here feeling her tighten around him. It was a few moments before he even felt the desire to move and then when he did, it was because of an overwhelming response to her squeezing and contracting around him. He lost all control and slammed into her, mindful only of maintaining the proper angle and keeping his firm footing.

Then she called out his name and opened her arms to him. He couldn't resist her beckoning arms, and his lips wanted desperately to crush hers under his, so he climbed up on the bed between her legs and with his hard thighs, he nudged hers even farther apart. Keeping his weight off of her, he repositioned himself and slid back inside her.

Her hands grasped his shoulder and back muscles and then ran down the length of him, coming back to the front so her fingers could splay themselves in his furred chest to tease his tight nipples.

With his hands stretched out on either side of her, he was like a Marine doing pushups. Very fast, very strenuous pushups. Then his hips lowered and he pumped even faster. With just his hips, he thrust into her so hard that he rocked the headboard against the wall. His tongue ran the circuit of his lips and revisited the taste of her still on them, and he groaned from the memory of her fulfillment. His hands on the bed clenched into fists, his jaw tightened, his eyes closed hard and his head fell back as he came into her, bathing her with his passion and the hot, liquid desire from his body. Deep into her body he thrust himself, one last incredible time.

He discovered that there was no word for the incredibly sated feeling he suddenly had. No word, except maybe exhaustion, followed by sleep. His head resting on the mattress, his lips kissing the side of her neck, he dropped beside her, mumbled something she couldn't begin to decipher, and fell fast asleep.

Michele turned on her side and smiled as she pushed a lock of dark hair from his brow. She was experiencing her own joy. Her own revelations. She'd called him Michael. Just split seconds before coming, in a wave of passion so intense she couldn't fight it, she'd called out his name. Michael. And then earlier, in that dream state, when she'd been in the chair, she'd called out his name then, too. And Lord, when he'd sucked her there . . . she'd practically screamed it for all the world to hear. Maybe she'd just have to consider reciprocating one of these days.

The significance of that would have been overlooked by many, but not by a woman who was convinced she was loving a different man. Now she knew that it was not Kevin she was holding on to. She had finally let him go. Now she loved Michael. Without a doubt, she knew she loved Michael. Michael, the father of her babies.

29 Weeks

THE BABIES BEGIN TO SHED THE LANUGO. THE DOWNY HAIR REMAINS
ONLY ON THEIR BACKS.

I spoke to Dr. Connor this morning. Wasn't there something you were supposed to tell me?" he asked as he buttered his English muffin across the table from her.

She blushed as she felt his irritation with her.

"Well?" he pressed.

"Yes, I guess there was."

"Something about considering weekly progesterone injections to reduce your risk of prematurely delivering?"

"He didn't say I had to. It was only a suggestion."

"A suggestion by a premier doctor in the field who knows what the hell he's talking about! His research on this damned near built Wake Forest for crying out loud!"

"I don't like shots. And he wasn't absolutely sure it would help in my case."

"I listened to you about not wanting me to monitor you, not wanting me to do weekly pelvics, but if you're not going to listen to the colleagues I send you to, I will strap you down and insert a speculum in you so fast your head will spin!" He took a deep breath, and started speaking again, this time slower and less harshly. "This morning, I will take you to the hospital with me, see that you have an injection, and arrange for you to come home. Is that clear?"

There was no way she could argue with the man-turned-monster sitting across from her, and she knew it.

"Yes," she whispered, and lowered her head to pick at her plate.

"Good, now go get ready, because I have to leave in ten minutes and it doesn't appear that you're going to be eating anymore anyway."

She slowly stood and slinked out of the room. Boy was he mad! She was truly glad that neither the kids nor Anita had been here to hear him yell and hiss at her. Was it really all that serious that she take these stupid injections? She hadn't thought so at the time, but she guessed she had made a huge mistake not telling him about them. She was over the hump, so to speak. The babies would be okay if they were delivered anytime now, wouldn't they?

Later that night, Michael came home to a house that was completely dark. Even the second floor had no lights on. He tiptoed to the master bedroom and saw that she wasn't there. Then he walked to the other side of the house to the guest room where she had been staying before, and there she was sound asleep on the bed, the covers cocooned all around her.

He stood in the room, and using the faint light coming in through a high transom, he looked down at her. So, she was mad at him, eh? Served him right. He had been a bit of a bully. He just cared so damned much about her and only he knew how tenuous this pregnancy was. Every day those babies stayed with her bought him more peace of mind. She couldn't know how much the idea of losing her petrified him with fear. If he'd known for certain that they already had the cord they needed for Amanda, he might have been tempted to terminate these babies when she'd lost the last one. She was not the best candidate for carrying babies. She could bleed to death so easily. It was one of the reasons he was sure a Caesarean was the only way to go with her. The labor process was going to be too much for her frail amniotic sacs and cords and the tightness of her womb, made even tighter with its reduced elasticity from the recent surgery, wasn't going to help matters at all. But she didn't know all this. She didn't know that this *had* to be her last pregnancy.

He walked over to the bed, bent and kissed her on the cheek. Then he went back to his room. If she insisted on sleeping here tomorrow night, when he got home, he'd carry her to his room if he had to, either that or sleep in here with her. Tonight, he'd let her rest.

30 Weeks

THE MOTHER'S IMMUNITIES ARE TRANSFERED TO THE BABIES.

Three days after Mandy, Sam, and Gabby got back from San Francisco, Mandy started getting sick again. She woke up one morning and you could instantly see that her skin had gone shades paler than it had been just the night before. As soon as Michael saw her coming out of the hall bathroom that morning, he yelled for Sam to get their coats.

Michele came running from the kitchen where she'd been fixing breakfast and as soon as she saw Mandy, she knew she'd relapsed again. Michael bundled her into her coat and carried her out to the car while he instructed Sam to hold onto Michele on the slippery drive. He cursed himself for not having put the car in the garage as he should have last night. Gabby had even reminded him about it; she had even offered to do it for him. Now, Gabby was hurriedly clearing snow from the windshield. On the drive to the hospital, Mandy kept fading in and out. She was suddenly so weak it was hard for her to hold her head up.

All day they worked on her, until finally, at seven o'clock in the evening, she started responding. The treatment this time was a transfusion, but even as some of her coloring came back, the dark shadows under her eyes continued to increase. The hematocrit verified that her red count was dropping drastically. The stem cells from baby Marci weren't working, or they weren't even there anymore. They'd most likely been eaten up by the disease before they could multiply enough to make a difference. Now the disease was taking an even firmer hold on Amanda. It was settling in to do its worst, to finish her off, and they all knew without being told that she was in a non-responsive relapse.

"I want to deliver now!" Michele screamed at Michael across the conference table.

He ran his long fingers through his hair and turned to look at her. She was distraught to the point of being beside herself. She was frantic with worry and scared to death for her child. He had to remember that, because all he wanted to do right now was shake her.

"It's too soon."

"How can it be too soon? Everything I read says the babies will live if they're born now. They might be small, they may need to be hospitalized for a while, but they'll be okay. I know it! We have to save Amanda now!"

In his exasperation, Michael ran one hand over his face while with the other, he stretched out his arm, hand open, to yield the floor to one of the doctors sitting at the long table.

"I believe Dr. Moore is right, Mrs. Moore. The babies need at least another four weeks to be healthy, two to be viable."

"Mandy may not make it four weeks!"

Another doctor piped up, "You know in medicine, we can't weigh one person's life against another's."

She spun on him, her eyes blazing fire. "This is my daughter! I did this for her!" she said pointing agitatedly at her large abdomen.

"Be that as it may, Mrs. Moore, we cannot jeopardize the lives of both you and your babies to save your daughter." This was the voice of the hospital administrator at the head of the table.

Michele was now shaking with rage, and Michael could see she was just a few minutes away from a complete hysterical breakdown. He rushed to her side and with his arm around her, he whispered, "Take it easy, honey. We'll figure something out."

She wrenched herself out of his arms and screamed at him, "Kevin wouldn't let her die! He wouldn't let her die!" Then she collapsed in a pitiful heap, and if he hadn't been there to grab her, she would have fallen right to the floor. He picked her up into his arms and carried her all the way to his office where he hurriedly had his secretary clean piles of patients' files from his couch before depositing her there.

"Can I get you something Doctor?" his secretary asked as he stood looking down at the woman he loved who was being broken in two.

"Yeah, some coffee, juice, aspirin, my Rolodex, and a few miracles."

"Coming right up."

Ten minutes later, Michael sat with Michele cradled in his lap and just held her as she cried her heart out. The churning in his stomach was worse than it had ever been, even during the most harried of operations. Her heart breaking was breaking his and he didn't know what to do about it. The phone on his desk rang and he eased her off of him so he could get to it.

"Dr. Moore," he answered. Then he listened and said "I'll be right there."

"What? What is it?" Michele asked. "Is it Amanda?"

"Yes honey, it's Amanda. The specialist I called in is with her now. I have to go talk to him."

"I'm coming, too," she said as she stood and wiped at her eyes.

He gripped her firmly by the arms and bent to look into her face. "No. No you're not. The last thing Amanda needs right now is to see how badly you're handling all this. You're going to stay right here while I go talk to him, and then when I get back, we'll make some decisions. Now, do I need to call security to keep you here or are you going to behave?" His tone was final and she knew it.

"I'll wait here."

"Good," he pronounced as he grabbed up the aspirin bottle. Taking two and downing them with the lukewarm coffee, he stared at her. "And for your information, Kevin wouldn't have had the first clue about keeping Mandy alive. Hell, look how well he did for himself!" He knew he was going to regret that outburst later, but he didn't care. She had made him angry with her insistence on throwing away the lives of their babies and possibly hers, too.

He talked to six specialists that day in a field so remote from his that it could have been a different science all together. The specialties of medicine were extremely varied and intricate. They were all lumped together under the general title of medicine because they all dealt with the human form. The surgeries he performed were a world apart from the sciences of the blood about which he had only a basic knowledge.

He arranged for a private room for Michele to share with Mandy and then he called on the expertise of his son. Sam had been doing the research on this for him. By now he was practically an expert in the field.

By midnight of the following night, he had a plan. He went to Mandy's room knowing full well that Michele would be there, and more than likely, wide awake. He knocked lightly on the door and then walked in. Mandy was asleep with her covers brought up to just under her chin. Poor kid. He knew she didn't like to have the covers past her shoulders, but her mother in her anxiety, kept tugging them up there. He smiled at the thought. Michele was a ferocious little mother, definitely someone to contend with when one of her cubs was threatened. He had to admire that, and even looked forward to her displaying that same loyalty to his twins.

His twins. He hardly dared to hope that all would go well and that soon he might be holding them lovingly in his hands. He looked over at Michele, who looked back at him with a wry smile.

"Hi. Boy, do I owe you a big apology."

"Yeah, you do."

"Well, you could be magnanimous about it."

"Not a chance. You ran me through the ringer yesterday."

"I know. I'm sorry. It was a very bad day for me."

"Yeah, you could say that. It wasn't so hot for me either."

"Well, sit down and take a load off. Sam said you've been real busy talking to doctors about Mandy. What did you come up with? Anything good?"

"Yes! In fact, I think you're going to be so happy, you're going to marry me."

"Michael . . . ." she said exasperated.

"Okay, a subject for another time." He plopped into a chair in the corner and waved with his hand to indicate Mandy. "How's she doing?"

"Better. Two doctors came in. One tried to explain something to me, but I lost him after the word injection . . . then he gave her one."

"And how's she responding?"

"I think her color's better and she seems to be sleeping happily."

"Happily?" he asked confused.

"Having sweet dreams, I hope. See how her lips curve into a tiny smile every now and then?"

He looked over and sure enough, every few moments her lips quirked into a tiny smile. "Happily," he confirmed.

"So what's up? What this new treatment Sam alluded to?"

"Shhh, we're tricking her," he whispered.

"What?"

"We're making her body think we have the right medicine, when really we don't yet."

"I don't understand."

"We had the lab people in San Francisco thaw out what remained of Marci's cord. Then we managed to extract some cells, dead as they were, and resurrect them using this new technique Sam found out about. Then we mixed everything with some fresh stem cells from a baby born here just yesterday. That was another contribution from Sam. He spoke to the Chief of Obstetrics while we were checking Mandy in and asked him to save a few umbilicals, along with releases saying we could use them."

"He's a great kid."

"Isn't he though?" he said smugly. "Time will tell, but I seem to have a propensity for turning out great kids."

"What about Stephanie?" she asked jokingly, and then was sorry that she had as she watched a look of longing cross his face.

"Yeah, Stephanie. She was great. Wish I could have kept her longer," he said wistfully. And even though she knew how he meant it, it was still like a kick in the gut.

As she watched the faraway look in his eyes clear, she mentally shook herself. He's not over her, she told herself, and he never will be. And here, I thought the only problem we'd have between us would be Kevin.

She cleared her throat, where a lump had settled, and asked, "So just what does this new treatment mean for Mandy?"

"We're hoping we bought you four weeks. There's no way to tell how much time she's got. Everyone's just guessing at three months. Her bone marrow will overpower these cells eventually, it's just a matter of time. If she can get the real treatment, where her body is purged before plentiful cells that are closer to her own genetic makeup are introduced, she may be home free in six to eight weeks."

"Oh, that would be wonderful!" Michele exclaimed and they both turned to look at Mandy just in time to see her have another "happy dreams" smile.

Michael chuckled and Michele sighed.

"Well, I guess I'd better get my butt moving and get on home," Michael said as he stood and stretched his long body.

"Yeah, and be sure to thank Sam for me, would you?"

"Certainly." He walked over to where she sat and braced an arm on each side of her chair. "When this is all over, we're going to talk about marriage again, and this time you're going to say yes. I hate going home to a house without you in it and I especially hate getting into a bed without you in it."

He took her lips with his and kissed her leisurely, letting his lips linger and his tongue wander. "Goodnight, sweetheart."

From the door he called back to her, "Get your feet up."

31 Weeks

THE BABIES' FINGERNAILS HAVE GROWN TO THE TIPS OF THEIR
FINGERS.

Mandy improved so rapidly that she came home from the hospital after less than a week. It was decided that she would not go back to school until after the babies were born. Michael didn't want to tempt fate by letting her catch anything as devastating as a cold or flu. So during the day, Michele tried to entertain her by playing games and watching videos with her. At night, Sam took over teaching her what she missed at school.

When Michael came home at night, he was often exhausted, but he was never too tired to massage Michele's legs as they sat on the couch and went over their days. He forced her to stretch out her calf muscles by pointing her toes and then pushing her heel forward so she could avoid the legs cramps so predominant in the last months of pregnancy.

They had talked many times since Mandy's relapse about the babies and how they would have to be delivered. Michele had finally agreed to the Caesarean all her doctors were recommending and Michael, unbeknownst to her, had signed on as her primary once again. Once she was sedated, who was to know? There was no way he was letting anyone else take care of her. In his opinion, most OB's fought harder for the baby than the mother, and that certainly wasn't going to happen here. The babies were crucial, but only so far as Michele's life was not involved. She had become the most important thing in his world and it scared the hell out of him.

As he rubbed her toes and stroked her arches, he asked her again if he could legitimize the babies before they were born by marrying their mother.

"I can't marry you, Michael. I can't be the second best."

"Just what do you mean by that?"

"You'll always love Stephanie the most. And I'd always feel that if you could choose, you'd pick her over me. I couldn't stand that," she said in a soft sob.

"Is that how you feel about me? Like I'm second best? That you'd rather have Kevin?"

"No. Of course not. It's not like that at all."

"So why would you think it would be like that for me?"

"You loved her so much."

"And you loved him so much."

When she didn't say anything else, he continued, "It's different with you. Stephanie and you are two totally different loves. Sort of like, one night you want filet mignon, and the next night you feel more like lobster. The love is totally *not* the same. So you see, you're not second best just like I'm not second best. We're the menu that's being offered now. If either Kevin or Stephanie comes back, then we'll have something to worry about. And as much as I love my brother, I know I want you more. So please, if he does come back, make him the salmon mousse and me the juicy New York strip."

"I don't like salmon."

"I know," he said as he took her into his arms, "not a hard choice, huh?" He kissed her deeply and then murmured against her ear, "The only woman I want is you. You, the mother of my children." He took her lips with his, capturing them and caressing them with his own. When his passion had burgeoned so much that it was visible in the way it tented his pants, he took her hand and placed it firmly over his erection. "If Kevin was here and you weren't, if this was his erection and he was with someone else, what would you want for him? Would you want him to be happy? Would you let him go?"

"Yes. I would want him to have a happy life."

"Then that's what you must do, too."

He turned her so she was lying between his legs, both of them staring up at the loft, his hardness pressed into her lower back.

"Mmmm, that feels good on my back. It's pressing in just the right place."

"Wait 'til you feel how good it feels a little lower. That's just the right place."

"We haven't done it that way yet."

"Yes, I know. I'm saving the best for when you're too heavy up front and the babies have dropped, which should be just about any day now."

She turned in his arms and looked up at him, "Are we talking about the same thing?"

"I think so," he smiled. "Woof, woof!"

She laughed so hard that the babies started kicking.

32 Weeks

THE BABIES ARE GETTING INTO POSITION. THEY EACH WEIGH ABOUT
THREE AND A HALF POUNDS.

Michael held her under his arm as they sat on the small love seat in Dr. Connor's waiting room. Michael had met her there for her appointment and now he was heading back to the hospital while she went home to check on Mandy.

"I spoke to the doctor who's going to take care of handling the cords. He says that testing each baby for tissue compatibility can take a week or two, and sometimes even longer. We aren't going to have that kind of time. We're going to need to know the day you deliver which baby's cord is going to be the best candidate. We might as well find out now if we've got one that's going to work. That means amniocentesis and marking each corresponding baby. Before you say anything, I know how you feel about invasive procedures, but this is Mandy's time we're talking about now."

"How do you mark the babies?"

"It's sort of like making a tattoo. We inject a permanent solution just under the skin, very similar to ink. We'll try to mark each baby on the butt, but if we can't, it may have to be on the leg or arm. If it's unsightly later, when they're older, we can use laser surgery to remove it, but we should be able to tag the butt."

"How will the markings be different?"

"By color. Each baby will be color coded and that color will follow through all the procedures. With two we only have to tag one, but it lessens confusion if they are both clearly marked. That way there are no mistakes."

"Sounds like somebody's done this before."

"Possibly. We're making some of this up as we go. But at this point, I don't believe we can afford to let Amanda's procedure be delayed. She can't hold on too much longer. Her blood count has started dropping significantly each day. It's good you've only got a month to go, because I don't believe she has much wiggle room on this. We're going to be cutting this pretty close."

"So will you agree to let them take the babies sooner?"

"No. No sooner than the 34th week. It's too risky."

"Why do you keep saying that?"

"Because it is. You're not a bleeder elsewhere, but you sure are a bleeder there. I know, I've been there. You bled like there was no tomorrow when we lost Marci. Thank God we were ready to transfuse you. You may need to be transfused again when the placentas pull away with the umbilicals. And God, the umbilicals. We'll have to work extra hard to keep them from bleeding out."

"Sounds like you'll have your work cut out for you."

"How'd you hear?"

"That you were the primary?"

"Yeah."

"I just knew you wouldn't have it any other way and Connor let it spill."

"I knew he would. The man's an old woman, can't keep a secret for the life of him." He bent down and kissed her hair. "So does it bother you?"

"No, I figure you've already seen my insides and you still want my outsides. What's one more time?"

"That's my girl. And God, I love your outsides," he said as he cupped her breast.

Dr. Connor came back out to talk to them about the tests and the tattooing. Then Michael arranged for her to go to the hospital and have everything done the next day.

33 Weeks

THE BABIES START STORING IRON IN THEIR LIVER. THE VERNIX
COATING IS THICK ON THEIR SKIN.

Three days later, Mandy went back into the hospital. Gabby flew out to see her. As soon as Mandy saw Gabby, she knew how little time she had left. She had heard how badly her blood was testing and she felt like she was one huge bruise. Everything was sore and it hurt just to lift the TV remote. Gabby tried to cheer her but Mandy was beyond cheering. She had decided that she didn't want to go see her dad quite this soon, but didn't know if there was a chance for her. She had never felt this sick and it never let up. It just kept getting worse.

"Gab, I'm sorry about those things I said about you and Sam. I was just jealous at the time and envious of both of you. Him for having your attention, and you for having a boyfriend who was so 'ga-ga' over you. You're the best friend a body could ever have and you deserve the best. In case I don't get to say it later, I hope you and Sam have a good life together and that you have lots of healthy babies."

"Oh, Mandy," Gabby said on a sob and came over to hug her through the bed rails. "You're going to get better, so stop talking that way. I fully expect you to be standing there right beside me when Sam and I get married, so don't make me mad at you by not showing up!"

"If I have any choice in the matter, you known damn well that I'll be there."

"Good. Enough of that drivel. Let's play some Sequence."

Gabby dragged out the game and Mandy shifted in the bed so she could see the board on the table. But before they could even look at their tiles and plan a strategy, Mandy fell asleep.

Michele was at the hospital with Mandy day and night, making sure she drank the necessary fluids, keeping her clean, and reading stories to her long after she was sound asleep. Michael came by to make sure her feet were propped up and to check on whether *she* was eating properly, but things were on a downturn for each of them. The further Mandy deteriorated, the more strain and agitation he could see in Michele. He had never seen her this despondent or so defeated. He sensed that she wasn't going to make it to the thirty-fourth week in any better health than she was right now, so he called the surgical teams together.

Mandy was barely conscious when Michele told her good-bye. If all went well, Michele would be able to see her in a few days. If it didn't, she might not ever get a chance to see her again. Michele kissed Mandy's cheeks and stroked her hair as tears fell from her eyes. "I'll see you in a few days sweetheart, and then we'll see who can get out of this place the fastest. I just know this is going to work, and you have to believe that too, honey. Please, for me. Please, please believe in me, believe in the babies. I love you, Amanda. Will yourself to get better for me. I couldn't stand it if you left me."

"You'll still have the babies," Mandy murmured.

"But they're not you, honey. They're not you. I love you. I don't want to lose you. You mean the world to me."

"Kiss the babies for me."

"You're going to kiss the babies for yourself. Don't think you're going to leave me with all those dirty diapers, you hear me Amanda Jean? Don't even think it!"

"I love you Mom."

"I love you too, Princess. Don't leave me."

Michael pulled her back by her shoulders and held her close to him as he walked her out of the room. "It's time to go now, sweetheart. Everything's almost ready."

Michele was crying so hard she was shaking with each sob. It broke his heart to see her like this. He felt useless, utterly and completely useless.

This woman, who was his life, was tearing him to pieces right before one of the most important operations of his life. He needed prayer. As he washed up, he recalled and recited every prayer he'd ever heard.

Even though Michele's recovery would be longer, Michael had opted for general anesthesia instead of the epidural. If anything went wrong, it would be far better for her not to be awake. And not knowing what he would be up against, he wanted to make damned sure she felt no pain; an epidural did not always deaden the entire area internally.

Michele's pubic region was shaved and a catheter was placed in her bladder to drain it so the bladder could be moved out of the way. Then her skin was cleaned several times. Her blood pressure was being continually monitored, and right now, it was starting to climb.

Delivery

EACH BABY HAS GROWN FROM ONE CELL TO OVER **200** MILLION!

It was hard not to be intimidated by the caliber of doctors he had assembled, but when he saw Michele's pale face, partially covered by the breathing mask, it became real to him. Real, yet surreal in a way.

Mechanically, he made the opening incision in her skin, forcing himself to remember his training and to be objective. Usually a bikini cut, called a Fanensteel incision, was all that was required, but because of Michele's special circumstances, he made a longer, vertical incision. If all went well, it would only be five minutes before he would be able to hold the first baby in his hands. In less than an hour, Michele could be in recovery.

He gently reached in and moved the bladder aside. The last sonogram, taken just a few minutes ago had placed the babies' positions for him and the monitors told him everything was as it should be as he moved the muscles aside and made the incision into the uterus. The operating table was dropped down so he could insert his hand into Michele's womb, then amniotic fluid and blood were suctioned out. He felt for the first baby's head. He was extra careful re-determining the position and fingering the cord. He was in the process of gently lifting the baby away from the wall of the uterus and closer to the incision opening the babies would be born through, when suddenly one of the heartbeats slowed erratically. He knew there'd be a cord problem, he just knew it!

Rather than waiting to find out the problem, and risk making everything worse, he used the palm of one large hand to hold the baby's head and with the fingers of his other hand, he readied to support the baby together with the placenta. He instructed Dr. Brarely to move in and push on the fundus, the top of the uterus, then he delivered the baby and the placenta as one, letting the cord trail in the opening. For a split second he allowed his mind to wander enough to recognize that this baby was his child.

Eager hands were waiting to take his burden and yet still hold it in close so he could quickly delve back in to see to the cord. There could be no tugging on this slimy, gray-white, pulsing connection to life. Michele's body couldn't take it and neither could Amanda's. He didn't know if this was the right cord yet, so he had to get it all and get it close without nicking the womb, but he was all but blind here and the cord length wasn't something easy to feel through the gloves. Then he heard the neonatologist holding the baby call out, "This is the red baby." Ironically, it was the boy baby. The blue cord was the one they needed the most. It belonged to the girl, yet to be born. Still, he was as careful as he could be to preserve it as well. He made the tiny cut, hopefully only a scant eighth of an inch from the wall of the uterus. He reminded himself that umbilical cord blood contained a concentrated amount of stem cells, but that the total volume of cord blood is quite small. He had kept as much cord as possible. Then the two other doctors moved to suction the baby's airway and to clamp the cord and make the separation of the cord from the baby. One down. One to go.

So far Michele was doing fine. Her blood pressure was still high, but not critical. And the bleeding was minimal. Nurses handed him gauze as he mopped and checked for bleeding. A nurse mopped his forehead—he was sweating like a son-of-a-bitch!

The anesthesiologist called out the blood pressure numbers again. All was well, still climbing, but not in the critical range. His hand slipped back inside her womb and he instantly felt the cord of the other baby pulsating under his thumb. The only problem was that the baby it was attached to had managed to wrap the cord over its head and through its legs.

"Damn! Cord's tangled. Two places . . . neck and legs. Going to have to cut it first. No, that won't work, it'll bleed out too much while I untangle the baby. I'll have to untangle it first somehow." He was talking out loud, but he was talking essentially to himself. "The key here," he said as he gingerly felt up and then down the length of the cord, "is what was it wrapped around first?" He stroked the cord as he had often stroked his chin, as he thought and tried to puzzle this out. Assuming the wrong thing would stretch it or cause it to break away and bleed from the connection point, the wall of Michele's uterus, or both. Then she would bleed profusely and the cord would end up hardly more viable than Marci's. Even with the eight units of blood standing by, ready to be transfused, she would likely die if she bled internally. Going for the leg first could cause just enough tightening to affect the oxygen going to the baby's brain. His baby. His little girl.

Holding his breath, he gingerly slipped the slick rope over the baby's head and instantly felt the slack that told him he had made the right decision. Pulling the baby's leg free was easy and just moments later he was lifting her out with her placenta and cord still attached. "Everybody ready? She's here!" His voice was joyous as he handed her off to the two doctors and the nurses waiting for her. Now, they were only waiting for him to make the final separation. Taking his scalpel in hand, he felt for the breaching point and was shocked to discover a stub from another cord. Momentarily, he was confused and uncertain about the cord he was touching with his fingertips, but then he remembered the first baby that had died. The stub, although just as slimy as the others, was prematurely small, not much more than pencil thin. He chose to leave it intact and groped to find the one he needed. He found the end of it, rechecked twice to make sure his fingers knew all they could about its position against the uterine wall, and made the cut.

As quickly as he could, he removed it and held it up for the suturing. Then it was off with yet two other doctors and Sam to do the miracle they were all counting on. Mandy would now be bombarded with low-dose irradiation combined with potent immune suppressants. The cells to be transplanted would be removed from the recently circulating blood and infused through a central venous catheter, this time in her neck. And while they waited the two to four weeks for the blood cells to reproduce, the engraftment stage, she would be isolated. It was almost a given that she would need several transfusions to replenish blood cells and platelets until the engraftment occurred. Her blood would be tested so frequently that she would think she was a pincushion on which phlebotomy students practiced.

His hand went back inside the womb to check for bleeding. He had removed everything intact so there was no fear of leaving any of the afterbirth. Somberly, he lifted out the baby that had died when it was only a few months old. It was little more than a flattened shell, appearing more like a onion skin that had been left out in the rain. A moment of sadness filled him as he realized this was his child he was holding, his child that didn't make it. Ever so gingerly, he placed it in the sterile stainless steel bowl that the nurse held out for him.

When he was absolutely certain Michele's womb was not bleeding, he sutured it up and proceeded to close the incision. In the background he heard the second baby being suctioned and encouraged to cry. It was heavenly music.

The series of incisions had to be stitched in layers. It was the most time consuming part of the whole procedure. He glanced at the clock on the wall. Fifty-five minutes. He made the final suture, tied it off and held it for the nurse to snip, then he gave one great heartfelt sigh and everybody in the amphitheater laughed.

"Congratulations doctor," one nurse called out to him and he smiled beneath his mask.

"Let's bring her to and get her into recovery so I can wake her up and kiss her silly," he said to the rest of his team, and together, they helped him take care of the woman who had just borne his children. The wonderful woman who had done such a courageous thing and snagged his heart in the process.

Recovery

Michael ordered the nurses to keep Michele heavily sedated for the first two days. He didn't want her to feel the pain of her surgery until he had some good news about Amanda. Plus, the neonatologists weren't allowing the babies out of the neonatology intensive care yet. Michele would normally have to wait a few more days until she could even be taken to see them, but he had a little clout and an orderly was on his way with a wheelchair for her. He knew she needed to see her babies, the two-day-old ones as well as the sixteen-year-old one.

The moment Michele opened her eyes, she saw Michael looking down at her wearing the biggest smile she'd ever seen on him.

"Papa?" she asked, with a big smile of her own.

"To the prettiest baby girl and the most handsome baby boy."

"Are they okay?"

"They are absolutely perfect!" he said and bent down to kiss her.

"Mandy?"

"Cord's doin' its thing. Her little sister helped her out big time. Her red blood count is already climbing up. They don't think she's going to have any complications. They're keeping close tabs on her and watching for any signs of rejection or chronic graft versus host disease, which I understand can occur anytime up to three, four, or even five years after the transplant. Sam tells me that because umbilical cord blood causes fewer problems in that regard and because the cells came from her sister, she has a greatly reduced chance of that ever occurring. Infection is the big thing they're guarding against, so you can talk to her on the phone, but you can't see her yet, except through the glass. Pretty soon now, she'll be bouncing off the walls she'll have so much energy. Right now, she's asleep. I just checked on her."

"It was the girl's cord, huh?"

"Yup!"

"Figures, the males never do any of the work."

"I beg your pardon? I think *I've* been working awfully hard lately."

She reached her hand up and clasped his. "I know you have, and thank you. Thank you for everything. My babies and my other baby's cord."

He bent down and framed her face with his hands, "No, thank you for *my* beautiful babies. I think I'm going to keep them."

"Oh no you're not. They're mine! Where are they? When can I see them?"

"They're ours. And you're mine," he said and silenced her with a kiss. "There should be a wheelchair here any minute. When it gets here, I'll take you to see them. By the way, do these babies of *ours* have a name?"

"Martin and Melissa."

"That's what I thought. What's with you and all the 'M's, anyway?"

"Michael, Michele, Martin, Melissa, and Mandy. We'll all have the same initials, M.M., except for Sam. We'll have to use his middle name, Maxwell. We can call ourselves the m&m's."

"Does this mean that we're all going to be a family and that you're going to marry me?"

"I suppose I should," she said teasingly, "I certainly don't want any custody issues."

"Would that be the only reason?" he asked.

"No," she said as she reached out to grab his hand. "You'd be a great father to the kids."

"One of us would have to get fixed. You can't do this anymore."

"Well, what happens if you get fixed and then one day you find someone else and you want to have a baby with her?"

"There will never be anyone else for me. Since you came back into my life, I've had blinders on. Besides, I already found someone who wanted to have a baby with me and we had two. Now it's time to ensure that we don't have anymore. I was very tempted to take care of the problem and never tell you about it before I closed you back up, but that would have been highly unethical."

"You didn't, did you?" she asked suspiciously.

"No, I did not. I do value my medical license you know. Even if you'd been my wife, I wouldn't have been able to make you sterile without your consent."

She looked thoughtful for a moment. "I know that I don't want any more children. Are you sure that you don't want anymore?"

"I'm quite happy with our little family of six. I'll arrange to have a vasectomy."

"Michael, are you absolutely sure? A younger woman would want to have a child or two."

He took her hands in his. "I don't know when you're going to come around and realize that there will be no other woman for me. You're it. As far as I'm concerned, I'm going to stay right by your side until you realize that I'm not going anywhere. When we're standing side by side watching Martin and Melissa graduate from Stanford, I'll look down at you, squeeze your hand and say, 'Now do you believe me? Are you ready to get married yet?'"

She smiled up at him and he could see tears filling her eyes. "Why?"

"Because I love you. You are the most caring and courageous woman I know, and you're one sexy babe. I can't wait to get you home so I can see how good your milk tastes."

Had she not already been sitting, she would have been forced to. Her legs tingled, her heart thumped, and her milk let down. She was in too much pain in the center region of her body to feel any warm fuzzy feelings there, but apparently her breasts were having no trouble responding to the thought of him suckling her. She hadn't expected her milk to come in quite so soon; but then, she'd been asleep while her body was readying itself to feed the babies.

She looked down at her gown and shook her head. "Now look what you've done! I'm leaking all over the place."

"I'll send for the babies."

"Tell them to send a mop and bucket while they're at it."

He chuckled and bent to kiss her lips. "Marry me?"

Just then a nurse arrived with the wheelchair. "Ready to see your new son and daughter?" she asked.

"Yes! And not a moment too soon, I'm like Niagara Falls here," Michele answered as she plucked at her damp nightgown. Michael bent and deftly lifted her into the chair.

"Do I get to go on a honeymoon?" she teased, looking up at him as he wheeled her down the corridor.

"Not for a while unless you want two little tag-alongs. And just where would you like to go?"

"To San Francisco to pack up my things."

"No way. I'll arrange to have everything packed and shipped. Let's go to Hawaii instead."

"With the twins?"

"With everybody. Amanda, Sam, Gabby. Hell, we're gonna need some baby sitters if we ever want to be alone again. And I *will* want to spend some time alone with you on our honeymoon. So, are you ever going to answer my question?"

They had arrived at the elevator and Michele busied herself with straightening her robe. They rode the elevator down two floors in silence. When the doors opened, he wheeled her down a short hallway and into a large room filled with tiny incubators.

She saw her babies right away. The two of them were in the same bassinet; one wearing a blue knit cap, one wearing a pink knit cap.

"Oh, Michael . . . . They're adorable!"

A nurse gently placed one in each of Michele's arms. Michele, her eyes filled with tears looked down at her babies. "I can't believe they're mine."

"Ours," he corrected. "You got an answer for me yet?"

"Yes," she whispered. "Yes."

She looked up into his face and saw that his eyes were filled with tears, too.

He wheeled her into a private alcove and opened her nightgown for her. Then he positioned each baby at a breast and knelt to watch as they rooted and then finally latched on. His eyes met hers and waves of passion passed between them as mother, father, and babies bonded.

"I'm not sure exactly when it happened, but I fell in love with you, Michael, and now I can't imagine my life without you. I love you, Michael. And I would be honored to be your wife."

Tears flowed freely down his face as he caressed her cheek. "Shelley, you have saved my life. I never thought I'd ever be this happy again. You've made me delirious with happiness and I can't wait to make you my bride."

"When? We'll never find the time to get married now."

"I say right now to the wedding. I can have a minister here in less than ten minutes and I can wheel you right into the chapel. But I think we're going to have to wait a few months on the honeymoon. You and Mandy'll both need some time to recuperate and the babies will need a month or two before they'll be ready to travel. Plus, I need to have the vasectomy and heal from that. What do you say to celebrating the day you called me and asked me to come back into your life, the day you asked for my 'donation?'"

"You know the exact day?"

"I do indeed. July 24th."

"Sounds like a good anniversary date."

"Sounds like an even better day to celebrate life and our new-found love with our new family. You really do love me?"

"Of course I love you. How could I not?"

"That's exactly what I was thinking, but it sure as hell took you long enough to realize it!"

"I think I loved you a long time ago, I just couldn't accept it. You were too good to be true. Still are."

"That's exactly how I feel about you."

Baby Martin lost his nipple and started to cry. Michael gently led him back to it saying, "Have your fill, son. Later, they belong to me."

Postpartum

THE TIME WHEN YOU DISCOVER THAT YOU HAVE NO TIME TO
YOURSELF.

Mandy was recovered as far as her doctors could tell. It appeared as if her blood was brand new and completely untainted by disease. She'd been on antibiotics since the transplant and would be for several more weeks. She'd had to have her immunizations updated as she'd lost all her former protection. She was also taking cyclosporine to prevent graft versus host disease or a rejection of the graft. Her immune system would take one to two years to recover but it looked as if she was going to have a long and happy life. She adored her baby brother and sister and if it appeared that she favored Melissa a little more, everyone chalked it up to them both being girls as well as blood-sisters.

Sam and Gabby announced their eight-year engagement. Mrs. Grissen didn't seem to mind her seventeen-year-old daughter being engaged at so young an age—after all, she was going to be marrying a doctor!

Michele and Michael settled into the chalet with their new brood. It was hectic when feeding time came as Michael was often demanding equal time. Michele reveled in her love for him and, even with four kids around, was lonely when he wasn't home.

On July 24th, the entire entourage including Anita and Gabby, arrived at the Denver airport for the first leg of their trip to Hawaii. Mandy's hair had grown in soft and curly and now that she was eating like a normal teenager, she was filling out quite nicely. She was going to turn some heads on the beaches of Kauai when she wore her new bikini, the one her mom had yet to see. Oh yeah . . . 'bye 'bye double A's, hello, double B's. She was indeed her mother's daughter after all.

When people discovered that Michele and Michael were on their honeymoon, they just stared at all the baby paraphernalia, the harried nanny, and the rambunctious teenagers, and shook their heads. These people were doing things just a little backwards, don't you think?

ML   9/04